Lydia

✩ ❤ ✪ PROM ☆ ❤ ✷

✦ ✷ ✦ PROM ✦ ♥ ✦

A novel based on the major motion picture
Adapted by Ellie O'Ryan ✩
Based on the screenplay written by Katie Wech
Executive producers Sean Bailey   Samson Mucke
Produced by Ted Griffin   Justin Springer
✩   Directed by Joe Nussbaum

DISNEY PRESS
NEW YORK

Printed in the United States of America

First Edition
1 3 5 7 9 10 8 6 4 2
J689-1817-1-11015
ISBN 978-1-4231-4564-6

Visit Disneybooks.com

★ ♥ ✦ CONTENTS ✦ ♥ ★

★ ❤ ✮ ONE ✩ ❤ ★

$\mathbb{S}$enior year. Second semester. Six weeks until graduation. Six weeks until the end of high school.

Three weeks until Prom.

For Nova Prescott, the counting down had started a long time ago—back in freshman year, on the very first day of school. Seven hundred and twenty school days, 574 shifts at part-time jobs, 423 chances to cheer for the home team, 285 multiple-choice tests, 119 lab experiments, 56 semester grades, 27 assigned books, 16 all-nighters, 7 college applications, 4 yearbook pictures. . . . It all added up to four crazy-busy, action-packed, drama-filled years of high school.

But there was only one Prom.

One night out on that dance floor under those twinkling lights, and all those memories would come into intense focus and completely fade away, all at the same time. A night worth all the effort and all the planning. A night worth holding on to.

As senior-class president and head of the prom committee, Nova was determined to make the prom count. In her heart, she knew that she owed it to everybody else in her class—one last night to make memories they would remember forever.

And Nova knew that she owed it to herself, too.

When the final bell rang at the end of the school day, Nova was the first student out of the door. There were only ten minutes before the monthly Prom Committee meeting began, and she had a lot to get ready.

At her locker, Nova spun the combination dial without even thinking, the numbers 32-4-19 burned into her brain from sheer repetition. She swung open her locker and looked at the top shelf with a smile of satisfaction. There it was, the big pink bakery box she'd smuggled into school that morning, completely untouched—and all thanks to the "lock" part of her locker.

In one fast movement, Nova wrapped the box in a

sweater and scurried down the hall before any of the other students noticed it. She peeked through the glass window in the door to the teachers' lounge and did a silent fist-pump of victory when she realized it was empty. Thirty seconds of microwaving later, Nova raced back down the hall to Room 109 and arranged three platters of warm cookies on the windowsill. She pulled a fat binder out of her bag and made sure that her pen had plenty of ink.

Then Nova sat back, exhaled so loudly that her bangs fluffed up, and waited for the cookies to work their magic.

Ali Gomez, one of Nova's best friends, was the first to arrive. She took one look at the cookies and said, "Butterscotch-macadamia chunk? Whatever you've done, you're forgiven."

Nova grinned. "I didn't do anything—yet," she replied.

"Come on, Nova, you can tell me," Ali teased as she reached for a cookie. "Oh my God, they're *hot*? What are you, Superwoman? How did you bake fresh cookies in time for the meeting? School, like, just ended!"

"I'll never tell my secrets," Nova laughed. "But I figured the hardest-working prom committee in the country deserved some cookies. You guys have totally earned it."

"Did someone say cookies?" asked a voice from the doorway.

Nova looked up to see Brandon Roberts standing there with the half smile across his lips that always made her heart skip a beat. She pointed at him. "Double-chocolate chocolate chip, right?"

"My favorite!" he announced as he strolled into the room. His sky blue polo shirt matched his eyes perfectly, Nova noticed with a quick, self-conscious glance in his direction; as always, every copper hair on his head was carefully gelled into place. "Thanks, Nova. These look awesome. So what's with the cookies, anyway?"

"Where's Mei?" Nova asked abruptly. "She's coming today, right?"

"What? Am I late?" Mei Kwan asked as she rushed in. As usual, she was wearing an adorably stylish outfit that only she could pull off. Her outstanding artistic talent shined through even in her wardrobe. "Come on, it's 3:01! I'm not really late!"

"Have one," Nova said as she pushed a platter toward Mei.

"Oh, yum," Mei replied, grabbing two. "Thanks.

So. Cookies? What's going on?"

"Well, as you guys know," Nova began, "Prom is only three weeks away. So I was thinking that it's time to ramp up our efforts. We might even need some extra help on the committee now that we're in the home stretch."

Ali whipped out her cell. "Okay, I just tweeted that there are HOT COOKIES in Room 109 to everybody following Brookside High," she announced. "If that doesn't bring people in, I don't know what will."

Suddenly, Nova got serious. "Actually, this is about more than extra hands," she continued. "Nobody knows Prom as well as you guys—you've all been here since day one. But there's just *six* weeks left to get everything ready. So . . . I think we need to start meeting weekly. Twice weekly."

"Twice a week?" Brandon exclaimed. "That's not possible. Not with student government and Model UN and debate and—"

"Look at everything we've already done," Nova said in a rush. "We have the theme. We have the location. We *finally* got our budget approved by Principal Dunnan and the school committee."

"So what's the problem?" Ali asked.

Nova ticked off the problems on her fingers.

"Posters. Tickets. Decorations. Photos. Prom Court. Advertising—"

"Okay, okay." Mei sighed. "We get it. And you're right. There's still a ton of stuff to do."

"We can have, like, subcommittees," Nova suggested. "You know, to divide up the work a little more. But I still think it would be really good to have meetings twice a week so we can check in. And help each other out."

When nobody responded, Nova picked up a tray of cookies. "And cookies! I promise, you guys, there will be awesome baked goods at the rest of the meetings."

"Hey, you don't have to do that," Mei said as she reached for an oatmeal cookie. "We don't need bribes to get everything done."

Nova smiled at her. "They're not bribes," she replied. "They're thank-yous."

"They look like cookies to me," came an unfamiliar voice from the doorway. Nova looked up to see Rolo, the most laid-back guy at Brookside High.

"Hey. Did you get my tweet?" Ali asked him, barely glancing up from her cell.

As Rolo shook his head, his wild blond curls bobbed back and forth. "I didn't hear any tweets," he replied.

♥ 6 ☆

"But I did smell some cookies."

"Help yourself!" Nova said brightly. "They're for members of the Prom Committee. Would you be interested in . . ."

"Definitely," Rolo drawled as he grabbed a handful of cookies. Then he shuffled over to a desk near the window and started to eat.

"Okay!" Nova said. "Let's split up this list of things to do. Posters, anyone?"

"I'll tackle posters," Mei spoke up. "Any special requests?"

"Cool," Nova said as she made a note in her binder. "I can only think of two requirements. One, they should really capture the theme. But not in, like, a cheesy or predictable way."

"So, Starry Night, without being too . . . starry?" Mei guessed, twirling a strand of glossy black hair around her finger.

"Or night-ish?" cracked Ali.

"Ha-ha," Nova said, rolling her eyes.

"What's your other requirement?" asked Mei.

"I really want the poster to be designed by somebody at our school," Nova continued.

"Ooh, like a contest!" Mei exclaimed. "Love it."

"And you better enter," Nova told her friend. "You're crazy talented."

Mei shrugged modestly. "Yeah, I can throw together some concept sketches. If you want."

Nova smiled, but she didn't say anything. She knew that Mei's concept sketches would be so good they'd look professional.

"Hopefully there will be something from the winning poster that we can use for the ticket design," Nova said, glancing at her binder. "Now, Prom Court." Nova turned to Brandon. "You want to tackle that with me? We need to come up with a nomination and voting process. I do *not* want a repeat of what happened last year."

Everyone—even Nova—laughed at the memory of last year's prom. The stories were legendary: voting for Prom Court took place at the dance itself, and the ballot box had been stuffed with hundreds of fake ballots. When all the votes were counted, Spider-Man and Mrs. Potato Head would have been crowned king and queen of Prom—if Principal Dunnan hadn't called the whole thing off. It was the first prom in the history of Brookside that didn't have a prom court, and Nova was determined to avoid another fiasco.

Brandon perked right up. "Yeah, I'm sure we can

come up with a completely scientific formula to make sure the voting process is legitimate."

Nova nodded and looked back at her checklist, missing the sly smile that Ali and Mei exchanged.

"Photos. We'll need an amazing backdrop for the official prom photos," she continued. "So we should all keep an eye out for—"

"I can do that," Rolo suddenly spoke up from the corner, as he brushed some cookie crumbs off his shirt.

Nova quickly covered her look of surprise. "Thanks, Rolo," she replied. "It needs to be really special. After all, these are photos that everybody's going to look at for years. And, um, the rest of us will keep an eye out, too. Just to make sure we have options.

"So this is a big one," Nova went on. "Decorations. Since the prom is in the gym, it's going to take some amazing decorations to transform the place. The last thing we want is everybody to get all dressed up for Prom, only to feel like we're at a basketball game. I know that it's going to take all of us to build them . . . but Mei, I was wondering if you want to design the decorations?"

"Is the sky blue?" Ali asked with a grin. "Are these cookies delicious? Are Mei and Justin practically engaged?"

"Yes, yes, and yes," Nova said, "but I want to hear it from her. Mei—is that too much?"

"Pffff," Mei said. "Not at all. I actually already started sketching some designs last week."

"Of course you did." Nova laughed. "Now that just leaves advertising . . . you know, getting the word out, making sure everybody knows how to get tickets. Ali, I was hoping you'd—"

"Absolutely," Ali said at once. "I'm thinking: slow buzz, teasers, maybe a trailer on YouTube, and a dedicated Twitter stream. Yes?"

"And we'll have posters, too," Nova reminded her. "So the last thing to do today is to schedule out the rest of our meetings. How about Mondays and Thursdays after school?"

"I can't do Mondays," Ali said, shaking her head.

"Thursdays are out for me," Brandon replied. "I'm Switzerland in Model UN, remember?"

"Tuesdays and Wednesdays are no good," Mei spoke up.

"Saturday and Sunday mornings?" Nova asked.

The rest of the Prom Committee exchanged a glance. "Actually, Mondays and Thursdays will be fine," Ali said right away, and everyone else agreed.

Nova grinned at her friends. "You guys are the best. I promise, it will all be worth it. Come on, take some cookies home, okay?"

"Nova, I'll e-mail you tonight about Prom-Court voting procedures," Brandon said on his way out the door.

"Cool," she replied as she closed the enormous binder and crammed it into her bag. "See you later."

Mei and Ali were silent until they were sure that Brandon was long gone. Then they both started to laugh.

"That was very smooth, Nova," Ali teased her. "I have to say, I'm impressed."

"What?" Nova asked as her cheeks turned pink.

"Oh, come on, like you didn't plan it?" asked Mei. "You and Brandon, working on a prom subcommittee, all kinds of after-hours planning, just the two of you . . . ?"

"Whatever," Nova said, laughing. "I just tried to give everybody jobs that they would like. That's all. You guys wanna do it?"

"And get in the way of all those opportunities for Brandon to ask you to Prom?" asked Ali. "No thanks. I could never live with myself."

"I don't think—" Nova began.

"Come on. We've both seen the way you two look at each other," Mei said. "It's only a matter of time."

"And when it happens, I'd better be the first to know!" Ali exclaimed.

"Wouldn't Nova be the first to know?" Rolo suddenly spoke up.

Nova jumped. She had almost forgotten he was there by the window, stuffing his pockets with cookies.

"Seriously, there's nothing to know," she said firmly. "I don't know who I'm going to Prom with."

She turned away and shot a look at Mei and Ali. Both girls mouthed "Sorry!" back to her. Obviously, *everyone* had forgotten about Rolo.

"Okay, thanks again, everybody," Nova said casually as she slung her bag over her shoulder. "See you tomorrow!"

As she walked outside to her car, Nova heard all the bustle of a typical weekday afternoon at Brookside High—the marching band running drills in the parking lot; the lacrosse team practicing on the field; the cheerleaders working on their latest gravity-defying pyramid. When she got home, there would be plenty on her to-do list: study for her trig test, read six chapters for

English, and finish her physics lab write-up.

But now, in the walk from school to car, Nova allowed her mind to wander . . . straight to thoughts of Brandon. Would he ask her to Prom? Was he waiting for just the right moment to make his move?

And—more importantly—if Mei and Ali had picked up on how she felt about him . . . had Brandon noticed, too?

CHAPTER TWO

The next night, Nova was typing about a thousand words a minute as she worked on her English paper for Mr. Geis's class. On her desk, a large iced coffee (extra cream, extra sugar) sat in a puddle of condensation next to a stack of scribbled-on note cards and two battered paperback novels. The caffeine-and-sugar combo was just what Nova needed to get in the zone; as her fingers flew over the keyboard, nothing could stop her.

Nothing, except for the *ping* of an instant message. Nova frowned slightly as the IM window popped up on her screen—until she realized who it was from.

Brandon!

BRANDON: Hey Nova, you there?

Nova took a long sip of her iced coffee before she replied. She didn't want to seem *too* eager.

NOVALICIOUS: i'm here. hi! what's up?
BRANDON: Just working on the voting regulations for Prom Court. What are you doing?
NOVALICIOUS: paper 4 geis.
BRANDON: Oh yeah? What's your topic? Word count?
NOVALICIOUS: comparing the "character" of the moor in *Return of the Native* and *Wuthering Heights*. i'm @ . . .
NOVALICIOUS: 970 words
BRANDON: Nice. I finished mine over the weekend. I analyzed *All Quiet on the Western Front*. 4200 words. Not counting footnotes.

Nova raised her eyebrows. It was so like Brandon to write a paper that was twice as long as it was supposed to be. She had to admit she was impressed. Of all her friends, Brandon was the only one who seemed to like—no, *love*—school as much as she did.

💜 15 ⭐

NOVALICIOUS: way 2 go! listen, i gotta get back to
this. C U @ prom cmte mtg on thurs
BRANDON: Hang on. I have a great idea for the
Prom-Court voting and I want to run it by you.
NOVALICIOUS: K. go ahead
BRANDON: In person, if that's okay. How about
tomorrow at lunch?

Nova blinked at the screen. Okay? Lunch with
Brandon was more than okay. It sounded amazing.

NOVALICIOUS: sure, i'm free
BRANDON: Excellent. Meet you outside the
cafeteria. Have a good night, Nova!
NOVALICIOUS: bye!

As Nova closed the IM, she noticed that Ali was
online, as usual. She quickly opened a new IM window.

NOVALICIOUS: hey lady. wanted 2 let u know i
won't be @ lunch 2morrow
ALIGOMEZ: boo! y not?
NOVALICIOUS: brandon asked me 2 get lunch w/
him!!!!

NOVALICIOUS: !!!!!

ALIGOMEZ: omg, he is so gonna ask u 2 prom

NOVALICIOUS: u think?

ALIGOMEZ: definitely! remember 2 act surprised

ALIGOMEZ: must b all those xtra prom cmte mtgs. brandon has prom on the brain!

NOVALICIOUS: yeah. i mean, we're going 2 talk about prom court. it's not, like, a date

ALIGOMEZ: whatever. that's not all u will talk about

NOVALICIOUS: :)

NOVALICIOUS: hope you're right

ALIGOMEZ: when have i ever been wrong?

ALIGOMEZ: i mean, besides those shoes i used 2 wear freshman year. the orange ones? those were so wrong.

ALIGOMEZ: wrong, wrong, wrong

NOVALICIOUS: LOL. gotta get back 2 my paper. C U 2morrow!

ALIGOMEZ: bye! remember 2 tell me everything!

Nova clicked back over to her paper and picked up right where she had left off, the keyboard clattering beneath her fingers.

But this time, there was a huge smile on her

face—and it didn't have anything to do with her typing skills.

"You look happy," a voice said from the doorway.

Nova glanced up to see her father, Frank, standing there. "Hey, Dad."

"Is that homework?" he asked, nodding at the screen. "Or something more fun?"

"Homework," she replied.

"That's my girl," her dad said. "I knew you wouldn't start slacking off just because high school is almost over. I knew you'd remember that your scholarship to Georgetown is conditional on final semester grades."

Nova secretly wanted to roll her eyes, but she just smiled patiently. "Of course, Dad."

"I'll let you get back to it," Frank finished as he ducked back into the hall—but not before Nova saw the proud smile on his face. She shook her head as she started typing again.

Sure, Nova could see how somebody might be tempted to coast through the final weeks of high school.

But she'd worked way too hard for the last four years to start slacking off now. In fact, she wasn't even sure she knew how.

* * *

♥ 18 ☆

Right before lunch the next day, Nova ducked into the bathroom. In front of the long, spotted mirror over the sinks, she applied some lip gloss and fluffed up her hair. She stared at her reflection for a moment: the smattering of freckles across her nose; her warm brown eyes, looking just a little bigger than usual thanks to a hint of eyeliner; her full cheeks that tapered into a delicate chin. Then, satisfied that she looked okay, Nova walked toward the cafeteria, making sure that she didn't rush. She spotted Brandon before he noticed her.

"Hey," Nova called, with a little wave. Brandon looked up from the book he was reading, and a smile crossed his face.

"Hey, Nova!" he said. "Thanks for meeting me for lunch."

"Sure," she replied as she stepped into the cafeteria.

But Brandon grabbed her elbow. "Not here," he said. "Come on."

With surprise in her eyes, Nova followed Brandon down the hall. As they walked, he unwrapped an energy bar and started eating it.

"The library?" Nova asked when they reached the double doors to her favorite place at Brookside.

"I thought it would be quieter," Brandon said as he

finished his energy bar. "Ms. Randall lets me use the Reference Room whenever I want."

"But you can't eat in Reference Room," Nova replied. "Or in the library at all, actually."

"Oh—yeah," Brandon said as he reached into his backpack. "Do you want an energy bar? I always have an extra or two. Or we can go back to the cafeteria, I guess. I just thought we'd get more done here."

"Um, sure," Nova said awkwardly as she took the energy bar from Brandon and ate it quickly in the hallway. Then they walked into the library, past the rows of tall bookshelves to a small room in the back—the Reference Room. As Brandon pulled out a chair at the empty table, Nova realized that he was right: the library was deserted. Nova inhaled deeply, smelling the familiar, papery scent of gold-edged encyclopedias and old books. Whenever life at Brookside got a little too complicated, Nova always knew that she could find a moment of peace in the library.

"Seriously, I don't even know why they keep this room around anymore," Brandon said as he glanced at the rows of yellowed books lining the walls. "Wouldn't it be more efficient to have, like, twenty computers in here?"

"Mmm," Nova said. "I don't know. I love the old books, you know?"

"But half this stuff is out of date, and the other half is available on the Internet," Brandon pointed out.

"I guess," Nova replied uncertainly. Then she changed the subject. "What was your idea about Prom Court?"

"Well, my first thought was that electronic voting was definitely the way to go," Brandon began. "One IP address, one vote. Done. But then I realized some people don't have computers at home, so they use the school ones, and it would be impossible to monitor voter fraud."

"Right. Of course," Nova said, nodding—and trying not to smile at how seriously Brandon was taking his assignment.

"And e-mail voting was out, too," Brandon continued, "since there's no way to keep people from registering multiple accounts. So, I abandoned technology and went back to the basics."

Nova waited expectantly as Brandon rummaged in his backpack again. Then, beaming, he pulled out a steel box.

"What's that?" she asked.

"A lock box!" he announced. "Imagine it: the entire senior class, voting simultaneously in homeroom. Preprinted paper ballots, one per student. Then, the *homeroom teachers* deliver the ballots to Principal Dunnan, who stores them in this ultrasecure lock box until the Prom Committee is ready to make the count!"

Nova started to laugh. "That's back to the basics, all right," she said. "I think that's how they did it back when my mom was on the Prom Committee!"

"You don't like it?" Brandon asked, and Nova could hear a note of disappointment in his voice.

"No, I do," she said quickly. "My only worry is that I'm not sure the homeroom teachers will be on board. It *is* extra work for them."

"Oh, I'm not concerned about that," Brandon said confidently. "If you and I go around to ask them? They'll be all over it. Also, Prom makes people do things that they otherwise wouldn't."

"Yeah?" asked Nova, raising an eyebrow.

Brandon nodded. "You just mention Prom and people get all starry-eyed," he said. "Even adults, right? I mean—I know for myself—"

As Brandon's voice trailed off, Nova realized she was holding her breath. She waited for him to continue.

"I joined Prom Committee because I thought it would look really good on my college applications," Brandon continued, looking down at the table with a smile. "But now—I mean, I've really gotten into it. Thanks to you. It's so impressive the way you've pulled this prom together. You've had this vision since the very beginning, and your dedication is so inspiring. It's really going to be a great prom, you know?"

Nova's eyes sparkled with happiness. "Thanks, Brandon," she said. "It wouldn't have happened without everybody's hard work."

There was a pause.

"Nova, I was wondering if—"

Brrrrrrrrrring!

A piercing bell sounded, signaling the end of lunch period. Suddenly the hallway outside the library was crammed with students, and the noise echoed all the way back to the Reference Room.

"Back to class, huh?" Brandon asked as he bent over to slide the lock box into his backpack.

"Were you, uh—" Nova began awkwardly. "What were you going to say?"

Brandon glanced up at her. "Oh. I was wondering if it would be okay for me to be a little late to our meeting tomorrow," he said. "I have Model UN, but I should be able to leave early. Honestly, Switzerland doesn't do much, anyway."

"No problem," Nova replied as she grabbed her bag. "See you around." She hurried out of the library, joining the crowd of students in the hall on their way to seventh period. Nova was glad that no one could tell how furiously her heart was pounding.

For a moment there, sitting so close to Brandon that their knees were almost touching, an invitation to Prom had seemed so close.

But now it felt further away than ever.

As Nova suspected, it wasn't easy to keep her thoughts off Brandon—especially with all the extra Prom Committee meetings, which meant she saw him even more than usual. Though pulling together Brookside's Prom was starting to feel like a full-time job, Nova wouldn't have wanted it any other way, especially since it kept her too busy to worry about things like finding a dress . . . or a date. The weeks rushed by in a flurry of caterer tastings, DJ meetings, decoration building, and a thousand other details that constantly demanded Nova's attention.

On her way to one of the final Prom Committee

meetings, Nova was so distracted that she nearly ran right into Jordan Lundley, the most popular girl at Brookside. Jordan wasn't popular because she was rich or connected or anything like that. It was because she was genuinely nice to everyone she met.

And it didn't hurt that she was gorgeous, with sleek, straight hair, enormous eyes, and perfect coffee-colored skin—with an absolutely killer fashion sense.

"Nova, whoa! Where are you rushing off to?" Jordan asked, her dark brown eyes twinkling.

"Prom committee meeting—sorry, Jordan," Nova replied. "I didn't mean to plow you down."

"No worries," she said, stepping out of Nova's way. "You're on a mission. I can respect that. Don't let me stand in your way!"

"Thanks," Nova said with a grin. "And while I must remain impartial, you and Tyler should know the queen's crown is silver and the king's is gold. So you can coordinate. I'm just saying."

"Good to know." Jordan laughed as a group of girls surrounded her, each one clamoring for Jordan's attention.

"Jordan, if Kyle asks me, we totally want to ride with you and Tyler!" exclaimed one.

"Jordan, the second you choose your dress you have to post it so none of us accidentally pick it," said another. "Wearing the same dress as Jordan Lundley to Prom—high school nightmare!"

Jordan just smiled sweetly as she watched Nova hurry down the hall. There was the kind of pressure Nova was used to—making straight A's, coordinating a ton of extracurriculars, heading up a bunch of committees. And then there was the kind of pressure Jordan knew all too well—dating the most popular guy in the senior class, juggling more friends than she could handle, knowing that everybody was watching her every move.

Neither one was easy to handle.

When Nova arrived at the meeting, she was surprised to see that Rolo was already there, grinning proudly. Mei, Brandon, and Ali arrived right after she did.

"We all know that Prom memories last forever," Nova began. "But we all want something we can take away from the night itself. Something that takes you back to those special memories . . . of course, I'm talking about the Prom photos! It's hard to decide . . . do you want to go with something that's simple and classic, like a plain color or pattern . . . or something that is uniquely Brookside?"

Deep in thought, Nova walked right past Rolo, who was trying to hang a roll of white art paper on the wall.

"Hey, I got that white background you were thinking about," Rolo spoke up.

A slight frown crossed Nova's face as she examined the paper, which was wrinkled along the edges . . . and down the middle . . . and smudged with dirt. . . .

"It looks a little . . . worn," she said.

"You know, I'm really into found objects," Rolo said. "So, the first place I looked was in the backseat of my car. And I found this big roll of art paper! I found some other things. . . ."

"Okay, great," Nova said hopefully.

"Um, there's this stuff I found from a play," Rolo continued as he walked over to a few theater flats. "This one's a riverboat. There's also some city. A mansion. And I thought . . . proms are fancy. Those might work."

"Those are from the spring musical!" Ali exclaimed.

"There's also some other stuff," Rolo said, moving on. He held up an American flag . . . a Brookside basketball championship banner . . . a periodic table . . . a ton of stuff that summed up life at Brookside—but had nothing to do with Prom.

Brandon frowned. "People are looking for that stuff," he said.

"Lucky we found it, right?" asked Rolo. "I thought it might work."

Nova tried to think of a way to let him down gently. "I don't think these really go with our . . . theme," she finally said.

"Nova, I actually went ahead and got a night-sky backdrop from the photography class," Brandon announced as he unfurled a dark screen spangled with tiny, far-off stars.

"That's beautiful," Nova breathed. She stepped closer to get a better look. "Thank you, Brandon."

Behind her, Mei and Ali exchanged a glance.

"I thought it made sense with the whole 'star' thing we're going for," Brandon explained, sounding very pleased with himself.

"Well, there's like a hundred stars on this flag here," Rolo pointed out as he shuffled through the various items he had accumulated. But Nova didn't even hear him.

"Couples are going to stand in front of this and take

pictures they'll look at for the rest of their lives!" she exclaimed.

Ali smiled slyly at Mei. "Well, we should really see what it's going to look like, right?" she suggested. She jumped up and started to position Nova and Brandon together in front of the backdrop, just like they were a couple posing for a real prom picture. "Mei, can you—"

Mei got it right away. She whipped out her cell phone and turned on the camera feature.

"Just like this," Ali said as she moved Brandon so that he was standing right behind Nova. "That looks really cute. Mei, are you—"

Of course, Mei was already snapping tons of photos. Next to her, Rolo started doing the same. Brandon and Nova stood together, with just a touch of awkwardness, and something else, too . . .

Maybe a spark of attraction?

With Nova's honey-colored highlights and Brandon's copper hair, they certainly made a beautiful couple.

"Okay, now move in closer," Ali ordered them. "Or maybe—turn and face each other!"

But that, for Nova, was too much—especially with everyone watching. She stepped away as a bright red blush crept up her face. "I think we have a pretty good idea now," she replied. "This looks good. Thank you, Brandon. I need to—go over some of the tickets and things now. Ali, I'll call you later—"

Out of Brandon's sight, Mei waved her phone at Nova and mouthed, "I'll send to you!"

Nova ran her hand through her hair and tried to focus. She could hardly look at Brandon, wondering if he had felt it, too. "Um, Rolo . . . you should really put that stuff back. Thanks."

"Sure," Rolo replied as he scrolled through his phone. "Do you want me to send these to you, too?"

"Posters?" Nova asked loudly. "Are the poster final-ists ready, Mei?"

Mei hurried back to the desk where she had been sitting and grabbed three poster mock-ups. She posi-tioned them against the wall, with their backs facing out.

"I narrowed it down to three," she explained. "Really, there are only three to choose from."

"What do you mean?" asked Nova. "I saw a whole stack of submissions the other day."

"Most didn't work," Mei said bluntly.

"Aw, let me see," Nova replied. "There might be something to them, right? Show me the runners-up first, then we'll look at the ones you picked out."

Mei gave Nova a look as she reached for her over-size art portfolio. One by one, she pulled out the rejects.

The first poster was a beautiful work of art, with a strange, spindly-looking man standing alone, holding a corsage. His eyes were full of tears as he stared at a lone star in the sky.

"Well, it's pretty," Nova said, tilting her head. "But it doesn't really say what's going to be *fun* about the prom. Anything happier?"

Mei showed Nova a poster that screamed pink, filled with hearts, rainbows, and big fat stars wearing big fat smiles.

Nova cringed just a little as she searched for something kind to say. "Nice, but we probably want something that doesn't turn off the guys so much. . . ."

"You want guys?" asked Mei. She held up an intricately drawn poster covered with monstrous, fanged stars on a killing spree, determined to destroy every single promgoer. Above the carnage, a headline declared: STARRY NIGHT: The Prom to END All Proms.

Nova waved it away, so Mei showed her another poster. This one had an image of Brookside High School at night, with a bunch of celebrity photos pasted into the sky above the school. Nova squinted at the poster as she tried to figure it out. "Why is Justin Bieb— *Oh*," she realized.

"*Star*-ry night," Mei said, rolling her eyes. "Yeah."

"Okay," Nova gave in. "Show me the ones you like."

One at a time, Mei revealed the three final posters. Each one was really cool in its own way, and though they were all for the same event, each poster was surprisingly unique. The Prom Committee clustered around Nova as she examined the finalists, while Mei tried not to fidget.

"Which one's yours?" Nova finally asked.

"I don't want to tell you," Mei replied. "I just want your honest opinion of these and then I'll tell you."

Nova smiled at Mei as if to say, "You're going to make this hard on me?" Then she turned back to the posters, considering them so carefully that she didn't notice that Brandon was standing right behind her. At last, Nova pointed to the middle poster. "The middle poster is perfect, but I'd like you to try out the font from this last one."

"Really?" Brandon asked. "I don't know if I'd do that. They're two different posters."

"Let's just try it out," Nova said. She and Brandon

stared at each other, then smiled at the same time. "We'll see who's right."

"Your call," Brandon replied with a shrug.

Turning to Mei, Nova raised an eyebrow. "Think we could make that happen? Just to see?"

"You got it," Mei replied.

"Hey, thanks for a great meeting, everybody," Nova said, turning to the group. "I'm so excited. It's really coming together, you know?"

"It so is!" Ali exclaimed. "Once the decorations are done, I think we'll be all set."

As the rest of the Prom Committee filed out of the room, Mei stayed behind to pack up all the poster designs.

"Okay," Nova said when the room was empty. "Which one's yours?"

Mei paused and smiled before she pointed at the middle poster—the one Nova had loved more than all the others.

"Why am I not surprised?" Nova asked with a grin.

CHAPTER
THREE

That night, Mei and Ali stopped by Nova's house so that Mei could show her the updated poster design with the font Nova had suggested. "Oh, Mei, it's perfect!" Nova squealed, clapping her hands. "I love it!"

"You were so right about that font," Mei replied.

"All right! Let's get this baby to the Copy Shack," Ali announced. "We'll run them off tonight and plaster Brookside with them tomorrow."

"Already?" Nova asked in surprise. "But Prom is still—"

"Just three weeks away," Ali interrupted her. "Come on, Nova, the 'slow buzz' is over. It's time to ramp things up. And seriously, once everyone sees these posters, school is gonna be jumpin' with Prom excitement."

"Okay," Nova said. "Let's do this."

The girls followed Nova outside to her car, and within an hour, they had a hundred glossy, full-color posters printed up and ready to go. "Wow," Nova said as she stared at the thick stack of posters. "This makes it feel so real."

"Not nearly as real as it's gonna feel when you see these posters staring at you from every hall at Brookside High!" Ali said. "Want to meet at school early so we can put them up?"

"Sounds like a plan," Nova replied. "Thanks, you guys. I'll see you in the morning." As she locked her car, Nova took another look at the posters resting on the front seat.

It was amazing how they made Prom seem so near.

Nova woke up early the next morning, bright sunshine streaming through her bedroom window. She couldn't wait to find out what everyone thought of the gorgeous posters Mei had designed. As she drove to school, one of her favorite songs came on the radio, and she started bopping along. She could already tell it was going to be a fantastic day.

And, to her delight, there was actually an open parking space right near the main entrance! Nova grinned to herself as she started to pull into it.

Suddenly, out of nowhere, some guy on a motorcycle cut her off, revving his engine loudly as he zoomed into the parking spot.

"Hey!" Nova yelled, slamming on the brakes and the horn simultaneously. She flung out her arm to keep the posters from flying off the seat next to her. "Jerk!"

The guy on the bike turned around and glared at Nova from behind his helmet. Then he gave her a dismissive smile and waved sarcastically as he tore out of her spot.

Nova didn't waste another minute. She zipped into the parking spot and jumped out of her car. Cradling the box of posters under one arm, she hurried into Brookside High. Ali was waiting for her in the main entrance, texting away. "He's so gonna ask you today," Ali announced as soon as she saw Nova. Brandon and Prom were pretty much their only topics of conversation these days.

"Don't jinx it," Nova warned her.

"Please. He will," Ali replied. "I saw the way you two stood together yesterday. Let me see your surprised face."

"Ali . . ." Nova began.

"Oh, here he comes!" Ali whispered urgently as she spotted Brandon walking toward them. "Be cool."

But Nova was already feeling flustered. "Breathing, breathing, breathing," she told herself in a quiet voice.

"Okay . . . almost cool," Ali cracked with a grin. "Don't worry, you look awesome. Bye!" She grabbed a stack of posters from Nova and hurried down the hall, still smiling.

"Wow," Brandon said as soon as he saw Nova. "Beautiful."

She smiled up at him. "Brandon . . . I . . . thanks, I mean . . ." Nova stammered.

"That font really works with the background," he continued, and in that awful moment Nova realized that he'd been talking about the posters—not her. "I had my doubts."

"Oh . . . oh! The posters! Right. Thank you. Good font," Nova replied, grateful that she had avoided making a total fool of herself.

Brandon reached out and took several posters from

the pile. "I'm gonna do the cafeteria," he announced.

"Cool," Nova said. But the minute Brandon disappeared down the hall, she felt herself deflate.

Then Nova realized that one of her classmates, Rachel, was standing nearby, staring at the posters in her arms. Rachel was the kind of girl who was so alternative she'd rather let all her piercings close up than show her face at Prom. Even so, Nova recognized the gleam in Rachel's eyes . . . that particular look of longing that just about every girl got whenever she thought of Prom.

"It's gonna be great, Rachel," Nova said temptingly.

Rachel smiled sarcastically. "Yeah, maybe I'll do something *fabulous* with my hair . . . like shave it off."

Nova laughed as she turned away—and spotted Principal Dunnan hurrying toward his office. Although he was in a rush, Nova knew from experience that that was the best time to talk to him.

"Principal Dunnan!" she called as she hurried after him. "Good morning. I just want to make sure we're still good for the forty high-top tables for Prom. I know that wasn't in the initial budget—"

"Yes, Nova."

"And I'm still gonna need the extra custodial staff the

day before to help hang the decorations," she continued.

"Yes, Nova."

"Oh, and we're all set with the extra security and parking, too, right?" she asked.

"Yes, Nova," Principal Dunnan said. "I received both copies of your revised schedule and budget."

"Excellent!" Nova exclaimed as a big smile crossed her face. "Thanks. Prom's gonna rock, you know."

"I know," Principal Dunnan replied, finally smiling back.

"Oh, here," Nova said, standing on her tiptoes to pluck a piece of lint off his jacket. "Much better."

Nova bounced off down the hall, ready to start putting up the posters. Then she noticed something. The motorcycle guy who'd tried to steal her spot was standing just a few feet away, putting his helmet in his locker! Without the helmet, Nova recognized him at once: Jesse Richter, the resident bad boy of Brookside's senior class. She should've *known*.

With a glint in her eye, Nova walked up to the wall next to Jesse's locker. *Slap!* She covered it with a poster, watching Jesse out of the corner of her eye. Sure enough, he glanced up with a look of annoyance on his face. With a flourish, Nova added an extra piece of tape for good measure. Then she spun around and walked away—but not so quickly that she missed what happened next. A gaggle of girls descended upon the poster, shrieking and squealing.

"Ohmigosh, isn't it romantic?" cried one.

"I wonder if Steve's gonna ask me," said another girl at the same time.

"Saw *the* cutest dress the other day!" gushed a different girl.

Jesse let out a loud groan. He could not handle being forced to listen to this day in and day out—it was way too painful. He grabbed the poster and moved it across the hall. The gaggle of girls followed without a break in their chattering.

The crowd around the poster continued to grow. From down the hall, Lloyd Taylor noticed it and made a face. "Ugh. Prom."

"You know, you could go," his sister, Tess, pointed out. For a freshman, Tess was really cool—and pretty popular, too—the total opposite of Lloyd, who'd perfected the art of geeky quietness back in fifth grade.

"No thank you," he replied, shaking his head. "Prom is like the Olympics of high school. You wait four years, three people have a good time, and everybody else gets to live on with shattered dreams."

"My stepbrother, folks," Tess announced to no one in particular. "Can you believe he's single?" Then she turned back to Lloyd. "Come on, you're a senior and you've never tried *anything*! It's Prom! Ask somebody!"

"Oh, sure," Lloyd said sarcastically. "Let me just pick a cheerleader from my speed dial."

"*I* have several available friends . . ." his sister said encouragingly as she gestured to a group of gangly freshman girls nearby. They were all staring at the poster with longing.

Lloyd winced. "I'm not going with a freshman," he declared.

"You've got no game,!" she replied. "Come on, if not for yourself, do this for me. I have to go to this school for three more years. Don't leave me a pathetic legacy. Have some cojones for once. Ask someone. And be creative."

There was a pause as Lloyd considered what Tess had said. Then she pushed on. "This is your last chance to make anyone remember you even went here."

Lloyd looked away. He hated to admit that Tess was right.

Slap!

At the other end of the hall, Nova taped up another poster, not far from Jordan's locker. The area around Jordan's locker was a great place to advertise *anything*, since Jordan was always surrounded by, well, everyone. An instant clamor arose the minute Nova hung the poster, and such a big crowd formed that even Jordan's boyfriend, Tyler Barso, had trouble getting through. He walked through the halls of Brookside like he owned the place, and everything about him—from his close-cropped hair to his brand-new shoes—projected confidence and style.

"Jordan!" he announced, flashing a charming smile at all the girls within twenty feet—and loving every minute of the attention. "My queen! Saw the posters and thought of you. And about a party bus."

As he leaned in for a kiss, Tyler and Jordan looked like the perfect couple: they were both tall and gorgeous, easily the reigning king and queen of Brookside High since their very first date back in freshman year. But even though Jordan kissed him back, anyone who *really* knew her could tell that something was up.

"Hey, Tyler," she said in a sugar-sweet voice. "Can we talk?"

Jordan twined her fingers through his and pulled

him around the corner to a quieter spot. The minute they were away from the other students, Jordan's smile disappeared. "What is *this*?" she demanded, swinging a dangly earring in front of Tyler's face.

Tyler didn't miss a beat. "An earring?" he guessed, still wearing that adorable smile.

"Very good," Jordan snapped. "Why was it in your car?"

"You must have dropped it," he said with a casual shrug.

"I could have . . . if it was mine," she replied. Her eyes were like ice.

"Wait, I know!" Tyler exclaimed, as a look of recognition—and relief—dawned on his face. "I drove half the girls' soccer team to Papa Gino's last week."

"You did?" Jordan asked hopefully. She wanted so badly to believe him, but this wasn't the first time something like this had happened. Still, Jordan figured—if you couldn't trust your boyfriend, who *could* you trust?

"Yeah," Tyler said, shrugging again. "And one of 'em must have had loose earlobes. I could track her down if you want."

He watched Jordan carefully as he turned on his million-dollar smile. "Now stop being crazy," he said gently. "You know you're my girl."

Jordan's face softened. "I know," she said. "You're right. I'm just . . . I'm sorry. I just want Prom to be perfect. It's our moment, you know? I want to be up there with you wearing those crowns—us, together, like people expect."

"I know," Tyler said quickly. "We're gonna go to Prom and—"

"Once you ask," she cut him off.

"Wait . . . what?"

"Tyler, you have to ask me," Jordan said. "You never ask anymore. It's not automatic."

"I know," he said again—more defensively this time. "I mean, I don't think that."

"Good," Jordan said, smiling for the first time since they'd slipped away together. "I can't wait then. I just know it's gonna be spectacular."

Jordan reached for Tyler's hand and pressed the earring into his palm. "For the soccer team," she said softly, just as a big group of her friends came around the corner.

"Where'd you guys go?" one of the girls asked, and in that instant both Jordan and Tyler snapped back into their regular selves.

"Nowhere," Jordan said brightly. "Just, uh, talking Prom." She slipped her arm through Tyler's and leaned up to kiss him on the cheek. Tyler got the message right away and wrapped his arm around her shoulders.

Everything about them looked perfect—just the way Jordan wanted it.

As Nova, Ali, and Brandon continued to cover Brookside with Prom posters, the excitement level reached new heights. Even the underclassmen were catching Prom fever.

"Megan Brooks went when she was a sophomore, so it can totally happen!" one sophomore girl said.

"Really?" asked another.

"Yeah. I heard when the guy asked her, she was so excited, she threw up," announced the first girl. "That's kind of romantic, though . . . when you think about it."

Her friend didn't exactly agree. "Ew!" she exclaimed, wrinkling up her nose. When one of the other girls in their group didn't respond to the grossness, she said, "Simone? Hello?"

"Hmm?" Simone Daniels asked, completely distracted. "Oh, yeah. Ew." But by the way she stared off into the distance, it was obvious that there was something on her mind. Something big . . . and serious. Her long brown hair framed her face, but couldn't hide the troubled expression in her eyes.

Nearby, two sophomore guys, Corey Doyle and Lucas Arnaz, were barreling down the stairs. Corey, as usual, was talking a mile a minute. Their friendship had been cemented over a shared enthusiasm for a particular band called Stick Hippo—an enthusiasm that was so intense it bordered on obsession. Of the two, Lucas was somewhat more successful at keeping it undercover. As for Corey, he knew that he'd lost that battle a long time ago, and was fine with letting his inner geek loose.

"Okay, you can add one musician to Stick Hippo— do you choose White Stripes Jack White, Raconteurs Jack White, or Dead Weather Jack White?" Corey asked.

"Trick question, albeit a brilliant one," Lucas replied right away. He didn't even need to think about it. "Change any one element and you will disrupt the balance of musical perfection. Stick Hippo must stay intact!"

"Nice. Exactly!" Corey said with an approving nod that made his shaggy hair fall into his eyes.

The boys stopped walking when they noticed the sophomore girls clustered around the Prom poster.

"Look at them," Corey whispered. "It's like they're in a trance."

Lucas, however, had eyes for only one girl: the beautiful Simone. Suddenly, she turned around—and caught him staring at her!

"Hi, Lucas," Simone said with a smile.

"Hiyou!" he stammered as his dark eyes lit up. "I mean, hey . . . there . . . you."

"Thanks for your help on the gravity experiment," Simone continued, pretending not to notice how flustered Lucas was.

"Oh. Yeah. Anytime," Lucas blathered. "Just think of me as your lab partner."

"You *are* my lab partner," she replied.

"Good point," Lucas said lamely. Even Corey shook his head.

"I need a serious cram session for the elements test," continued Simone. "I don't even know the atomic weight of carbon."

"Twelve!" Corey spoke up.

"Thanks, Corey," Lucas said, shooting him a look.

"Excluding isotopes," he added.

"Thank you," Lucas said firmly.

"See you in class," Simone said with a little wave.

Thirty seconds after she walked away, Corey pounced. "Dude! She wants you!"

"Yeah, right," Lucas replied, watching Simone as she moved down the hall.

"I'm serious," his friend insisted. "That was *almost* a triumphant Hendrix at Woodstock moment!"

"More like the Stones at Altamont," Lucas laughed.

"Ooh, tragic," Corey said. "But not true. She's into you."

"You're crazy," Lucas said, shaking his head. "She doesn't wanna go out with me. She wants—*that*." He pointed at the Prom poster. "I've got nothing to offer. No car, no cool parties, no currency at all. I mean, what am I gonna do, ask her to join our Stick Hippo fan club?"

Corey's mouth dropped open. "She's down with the Hippo?" he gasped. "She's a Hippo-critter?"

"First of all, that's not even a thing," Lucas said. "And second, no one at this school even knows who Stick Hippo is. Except us."

"Our fan site had one hit last week!" Corey argued.

"It was probably your mom . . . again," said Lucas.

Corey couldn't disagree with that. The boys continued down the hall, right past the pillar that Nova and Mei were plastering with posters, moving together like clockwork to cover every side.

"I love us," Mei declared as they examined their work.

Right then, Mei's boyfriend, Justin, arrived. "Nice tee," he said casually when he noticed the cute little Mickey Mouse T-shirt that was part of Mei's eclectic outfit. "So where are you going to college next year?"

"University of Michigan," Mei replied, just as casually. "I hear the guys there are really cute."

Even Nova had to roll her eyes at this routine. It was no secret that both Mei and Justin would be attending the University of Michigan next year. That had been their plan since they were sophomores.

As Justin leaned in to give Mei a kiss—a *real* kiss, on the mouth, full of love—Nova slipped away, carrying the last two posters under her arm. Even though they had been dating since middle school, Mei and Justin were still a completely adorable couple. But sometimes, seeing them together just reminded Nova that she didn't have a boyfriend who loved her like that.

She shook it off and focused on the last posters under her arm—just two left! Ali had been right. The posters all over Brookside truly did make Prom seem more real than ever.

Back down the hall, Justin and Mei broke apart. "Prom. Huh," Justin said, still teasing. "Who do you think I should ask to that? You got a friend, maybe?"

Mei pretended to glare at him. Then she reached up and ripped off his hat.

"Hey, gimme my hat!" Justin yelled.

"Uh-uh," she replied, holding it just out of his reach.

"Oh, it's on!" he announced as he wrapped his arms around her.

Nova could still hear them laughing as she mounted the next-to-last poster on the door to the main office. She admired the perfect placement in such a high-traffic area, then turned around to head to her locker . . . just in time to miss Jesse Richter walk up behind her. He rolled his eyes at the sight of yet another poster.

Then he swung open the door to the office and walked inside with the kind of attitude that comes naturally to someone who's been sent to the principal on a weekly basis . . . for four long years.

"Hey, Rhoda," Jesse said, his dark eyes glinting with mischief as he leaned over the secretary's desk. "I turned eighteen last week. You know what that means, right?"

Rhoda had worked at Brookside High for a long time. She'd seen Jesse's type come and go so often that she didn't even look up from her computer. "They can try you as an adult?" she guessed.

Jesse clapped a hand over his chest. "Rhoda, you break my heart!" he announced. "It means we can finally run away together!"

Rhoda did everything in her power not to smile.

"You and me. The open road. You can leave Dunnan and all this behind," Jesse continued, staring out the plate-glass window behind Rhoda at the beautiful spring day.

At that moment, the door to Principal Dunnan's office banged open. He grabbed two files off Rhoda's desk and rubbed his temples. Then he noticed Jesse.

"Jesse Richter," Mr. Dunnan sighed. "Great. Let's make this quick."

Jesse followed Principal Dunnan into his office and settled into his favorite chair. He leaned back with his hands behind his head, waiting for the moment he could get up and walk out.

"Richter, Richter, Richter," Principal Dunnan said as he shuffled through a mountain of papers and folders. Then he found Jesse's file—the thickest one on his desk—and flipped it open. "Okay, let's see," he said as he scanned the pages. "You've cut last period every Tuesday for four weeks."

For the first time, Principal Dunnan glanced up from his cluttered desk and looked straight at Jesse. His face was not happy. "You know what that means?"

"I'm consistent?" Jesse cracked.

But the principal didn't laugh. He didn't even smile.

"It means you've racked up the maximum absences allowable by law," he said loudly. "You do realize you're only cheating yourself."

"You know, I had a talk with myself and it turns out, I'm okay with that," Jesse said with a grin that infuriated the older man.

"This isn't a joke," he snapped. "This is your final warning. I've had you under my watchful eye since you got here, and you've been nothing but trouble—no regard for rules, rotten attitude, hostile to other students . . ."

"Have you *met* the other students?"

"Look, I don't have time for this," Principal Dunnan said angrily. "We've been having this conversation for four years, so I'll make it real simple. After graduation, everything gets a lot better. I go on summer vacation, and you disappear from here forever. You wanna do that with a diploma? That's up to you. But either way, you're not my problem anymore. A few more weeks, Richter, think you can handle that?"

"Oh, don't worry," Jesse said, his voice cutting. "I'll be sure to leave the place in one piece for you. 'Cause in September, you'll be *right back here.*"

"Get to class," Principal Richter ordered.

Jesse didn't need to be told twice, but he took his time easing out of the chair and leaving the cramped room. He knew all the ways to infuriate the authorities at Brookside High.

Especially Principal Dunnan.

For the rest of the day, everything at Brookside seemed amplified—the hallway chatter was louder, the passing periods seemed shorter, and the gossip zipped from phone to phone faster than ever. It was like open season for Prom, and the only rule was this: ask or be asked. Or watch from the sidelines.

With all the extra excitement and activity, the only private place Tyler could find for his very important meeting was the janitor's closet on the second floor. Crammed between a dusty broom and a shelf of nasty cleaning supplies, he looked uncomfortable. But that didn't stop him from saying what was on his mind. "I just had to talk to you," he began. "I've been thinking about you so much. Plus, I had to give this back to you."

Tyler searched in his pocket for something, muttering under his breath as he knocked his elbow into the wall. Then, he held out his hand to the beautiful girl sitting across from him. Something glittered in his palm:

the earring Jordan had found in his car. He had that look on his face, the one he always got just before he leaned in to kiss his girlfriend.

But it wasn't Jordan standing across from him.

It was Simone!

With a troubled look on her face, Simone took the earring and slipped it into her own pocket. "Tyler . . ." she said. "I . . . can't . . ."

He pushed aside a few mops to move closer to her. "You are so beautiful it makes me nervous just to be around you."

Simone's shoulders stiffened. It was so hard to pull away when all she wanted was to lean in closer. This was Tyler. Handsome, older, popular Tyler. Tyler that she had been crushing on since freshman year. "I told you I couldn't do this anymore," she said firmly. "You said that it was over between you and Jordan. I never would've gone out with you!"

"Look, I'm sorry, okay?" Tyler replied, and he sounded like he really meant it. "But the truth is, it's been over between me and Jordan for a long time."

"*Over* over?" Simone asked, letting just a glimmer of hope into her heart.

"Yeah," he said with a shrug.

♥ 55 ☆

"So you're not asking her to Prom," she said.

"I—" Tyler said awkwardly. "Well, yeah, I am . . ."

That was all Simone needed to hear. She pushed past him toward the door, but Tyler spoke fast. There was something about his voice that made her pause.

"What am I supposed to do?" he asked. "I can't just dump her right before Prom, it would be devastating. I'm not a complete jerk, you know."

There was a long silence.

"What does all this stuff have to do with me?" she finally said.

"Everything," Tyler exclaimed. "It wasn't until I met you that I realized how unhappy I was. I know I don't deserve a girl like you, but I can't be myself with anyone else. This just feels so right."

"*This* feels right?" Simone asked in amazement, gesturing around her. "*This* is a closet!"

"Please try to understand," Tyler pleaded. "I want to be with you, but I'm trying to do the right thing."

Simone met his eyes at last. "So am I, Tyler," she replied.

Then she pushed open the door and walked away. Popular or not, Simone was better than this.

*   *   *

After school that day, the Prom Committee met to put the finishing touches on all the decorations they had made over the last few weeks. The barely used storage shed at the back of the school was brimming with shiny metallic stars, dozens of star-spangled centerpieces, an enormous gothic-looking tree, and—best of all—the celestial fountain that they had built. Even the dusty, dark storage shed was transformed by the elegant decorations. Nova could hardly wait to see them in the gym, where they would be augmented by dramatic lighting and fabulous music. The rest of the Prom Committee seemed as awed as she was as they surveyed all they had done.

"Are we . . . done?" Brandon finally asked.

"What?" Rolo said.

"No . . . no way," Ali replied, hardly daring to believe it. She snuck a glance at Nova. "Nova?"

Nova pursed her lips, deep in thought. "Well . . ." she began. "That was the last of the decorations, but we still need to figure out the floor plan and come up with a schedule of who's selling tickets, and of course count all the votes for king and queen, and . . ."

Nova's voice trailed off as she looked at her friends. They really, really, *really* wanted to be done.

"But you know what?" she asked brightly. "I can totally do all that stuff later. I got it. No problem. You guys . . . are done!"

"Yes! Awesome!" Ali and Mei cheered.

"Thank God," Brandon said with a grin of relief.

There were high-fives all around as the Prom Committee celebrated the end of weeks—no, *months*—of hard work.

Nova flashed them all an enormous smile. "You guys really are the best," she said sincerely. "In three weeks, Starry Night is gonna be Brookside's best Prom ever!"

"Our theme is Starry Night?" Rolo asked innocently.

Everyone stared at him in disbelief.

"Uh, yeah," Nova said, wondering if he was joking.

"Cool," Rolo replied, nodding his head.

"I can't thank you guys enough for all the work you've done," Nova continued. "But when those couples walk through the door and see how perfect it is, it's gonna be so worth it. Plus, you get free Prom tickets, so that doesn't suck, right?"

Everyone laughed as Nova passed out envelopes, each containing a pair of tickets. Ali's eyebrows shot up as she noticed how carefully Rolo tucked the tickets into his grubby-looking backpack.

"Sooooo, Rolo," she said. "Who're you gonna take to Prom?"

"My girlfriend," he replied matter-of-factly.

"Oh, right," Ali said with the hint of a smirk. "Of course. Your 'girlfriend.' Who doesn't go here."

"Yeah," Rolo said.

"And . . . what's her name again?" asked Ali.

Rolo's eyes darted back and forth, almost as if he were trying to think up a name. "It's . . . Athena."

"Athena," Ali repeated. "That's . . . unique."

"She's Greek," said Rolo.

"Uh-huh," Ali said, enjoying herself more every minute. "And where does she live?"

"Canada," Rolo said.

"She's Greek-Canadian?"

"There's a very vibrant Greek culture in Canada," Rolo told her.

Ali just shook her head and grinned. She had learned not to pay too much attention to Rolo's weird remarks.

Just then, the double doors to the shed opened, spilling in bright afternoon sunlight. It was Justin. He came up behind Mei and wrapped her in a big hug.

"Hey!" she said, surprised. "What are you doing here?"

"Come with me," Justin said mysteriously as he took her hand and pulled her out of the shed. He led her back into school, all the way to the dark and quiet auditorium, where he placed her in the center of the front row.

"What's going on?" Mei asked curiously.

"One second," Justin promised as he disappeared into the darkness. Suddenly, a brilliant spotlight illuminated the edge of the stage, where an enormous wooden *P* stood. Justin's voice echoed over the sound system.

"*P* is for the paralyzing crush I had on the beautiful new girl in my math class in eighth grade," he began. "Her name was Mei and she was awesome."

Mei started to laugh as the spotlight went out. Then another spotlight whooshed on, lighting up the letter *R*.

"*R* is for the really long time it took me to finally get up the nerve to ask her out," Justin said.

The spotlight went dark for a moment, then shined on the letter *O*.

"*O* is for the only girl I've ever called my girlfriend," Justin continued. "And the only one I ever want to."

There was another moment of total darkness, and then the last letter—*M*—was illuminated.

"And *M*, well, that's for Michigan, of course," Justin

finished. "Go Blue. Because that's where the next chapter starts. But I'm getting ahead of myself. Because before graduation, and college, and the rest of our lives together, there's something I need to ask."

Everything went dark again. But this time, when the lights came on, the entire stage glowed, all four letters spelling out the word *PROM*. Justin walked onstage and stood next to the *M*, holding a sign with a big question mark on it.

In the front row, Mei's heart melted. "Yes!" she exclaimed, scrambling out of her seat and running onto the stage. She threw herself into Justin's arms and kissed him.

Back at the storage shed, the other members of the Prom Committee left one by one, moving on to homework, dinner, and some well-earned downtime. At last, only Nova and Brandon were left. As she pulled the double doors closed, Nova could tell he was right behind her; there was a heaviness to the air, a feeling of expectation surrounding them that made her pulse start to race. Suddenly, she wondered if Ali's prediction in the hallway that morning was about to come true.

Was Brandon about to make his move?

Was Nova about to be asked to Prom?

"Looks like it's just us," he said quietly.

"Yeah," Nova replied, looking directly into his eyes for a moment longer than she normally would have dared.

"Do you have a minute?" he asked. "I was hoping to talk to you alone."

"Sure," Nova said. "Just one sec." She ducked back into the shed and, out of Brandon's view, fluffed up her hair and applied a quick coat of lip gloss. She didn't have a mirror, but it would have to be enough. "Surprise face, surprise face," she reminded herself in a whisper.

When she slipped back out of the shed, Nova's lips parted into a smile. "What'd you want to talk about?"

They started walking together toward the parking lot, past the athletic field where the cheerleaders were still practicing, with Jordan leading them in a brand-new routine.

"It's about Prom," Brandon began, and he suddenly stopped walking. He turned so that he faced Nova.

"Oh?" she asked.

"It's right around the corner, as you know . . ." continued Brandon.

"Is it?" Nova asked, wishing that she'd practiced her

surprise *voice* as well as her surprise face. Behind them, the cheerleaders formed a pyramid.

"And, we've been working together on the Prom Committee for several months," Brandon pointed out.

"That's true," Nova said.

"Which has led to what I would describe as a very cooperative acquaintance," he went on.

Nova started to wonder if she was wrong about this moment. "Uh-huh." Her eyes flickered over toward the field, where a guy was leading a blindfolded girl right over to the cheerleaders' pyramid. She clutched his hand, laughing, trusting him completely to guide her over any bumps or potholes in her way.

"And, since we're on the committee, I think it's a good idea for us to arrive a little early on Prom night," Brandon droned on. "Make sure everything's copacetic."

"I suppose that make sense," Nova said, still watching the cheerleaders out of the corner of her eye.

"So, driving-wise, we should go together," Brandon finished at last.

Nova blinked. "You want to . . ."

"Carpool."

"Right."

"Lessen our carbon footprint. Plus people get so

carried away with the prom-date thing," Brandon said, leaning back. "I say, why not be practical about it. You know?"

Nova watched his face carefully, trying to figure out if this was some kind of joke.

On the field, the cheerleaders—still in pyramid formation—held up giant, lettered placards that read

The boy untied the girl's blindfold. She saw the message, shrieked, and jumped into his arms, as the cheerleaders yelled and shook their pom-poms. It looked *really* fun.

Nova forced herself to focus on Brandon's words.

"No drama," he was saying. "An arrangement that's one hundred percent mutually beneficial."

"I . . ."

"Is that a yes?" he asked.

In the silence that followed Brandon's question, Nova realized that he was waiting for an answer. Her face was aching from the fake smile plastered across it. She tried to snap back to reality. "Um, well, Brandon, I—" she said, struggling to find the right words. Nova cleared her throat. "I'd be honored."

"Great!" he said, grinning so genuinely that Nova wondered for a brief moment if he really did want to go to Prom with her as more than just friends . . . if Brandon's awkward "ask" was actually concealing something more than just a very businesslike arrangement.

"Yeah, it is," Nova replied.

"Oh, here," Brandon said, rummaging in his backpack. "Just in case we end up having to meet there or something." He held out one of his two Prom tickets.

Nope. It was all business.

Nova hesitated for only a moment before she forced herself to accept it. And she kept smiling, too.

Even though it was the toughest performance of her life.

CHAPTER
✦ ✦ FIVE ✦ ✦

On his motorcycle, Jesse roared away from Brookside High as fast as he could without getting stopped by the cops. The feel of the wind blowing on his face, the heat the of sun beating down on his back, almost made him want to risk it. But Jesse knew that a speeding ticket was about the last thing he could afford right now. So he stayed within the speed limit—but just barely.

Several minutes later, Jesse pulled up in front of a public elementary school, where a group of seven-year-olds ran and played on the grassy lawn near the flagpole. Jesse revved the engine twice—their usual signal. But the kids were so loud that no one even noticed him.

"Let's go, Charlie!" Jesse yelled from under his helmet.

One of the boys looked up and waved at Jesse with such exuberance that Jesse grinned, as he always did when he picked up his younger brother from school. In moments, Charlie jumped on the back of the bike and fastened his helmet. Then they zoomed off toward home, a small house that was well-loved by the small family that lived there.

The minute Jesse cut the engine, Charlie started rambling about his day in first grade. "And Ethan got to be line leader because it was his birthday. But my birthday's in July—which is totally unfair," he said.

"Totally," Jesse agreed as he parked the bike.

"Every summer birthday gets celebrated on one day at the end of the school year!" his brother complained. "And there are, like, six of us."

Jesse shook his head in mock outrage.

"And they made Mike S. line leader first and his birthday isn't even until August so I said . . . Mom!" Charlie yelled suddenly as he caught a glimpse of their mother, still wearing her waitress uniform. He scrambled into the kitchen and gave her a huge hug, grinning from ear to ear. Ever since the boys' dad had left, Sandra worked so much that she usually got home just before Charlie's bedtime. And ever since Jesse had gotten an after-school job, it was rare for the three of them to be together in the middle of the day, but they were tighter than ever thanks to the struggles they faced.

Jesse hung back, watching from the doorway. "Hey. What are you doing home?"

"The place was dead," Sandra replied, grinning at her sons. "Lou gave me the afternoon off. I actually get to see my kids!"

"Cool!" cheered Charlie.

"And look what came in the mail!" their mom continued. She held up a cap and gown, beaming with a proud smile that was the real reason—the only reason—that Jesse even put up with Brookside High.

"Wanna try them on?" Sandra asked eagerly.

Jesse shrugged. "Nah. Actually, since you're gonna be here, I can call work, see if I can pick up some extra hours," he said.

"Sweetie, let's all take the night off," Sandra suggested, the hint of a frown on her face.

But Jesse was already heading for his room. As he passed the door to the basement, though, he froze.

"Who keeps opening this door?" Jesse asked loudly, glancing back at the kitchen. "Nothing but garbage down there."

He slammed the door shut and continued down the hall to his bedroom as if nothing had happened. But there was one change about him that was hard to miss: the tension in his whole body. Jesse hadn't been so annoyed since he'd sat across from Principal Dunnan that morning. It bothered him—a lot—to think that somebody had been poking around in the basement.

It was better to forget all about everything that was stored there.

Across town, Nova arrived at the garage where her dad worked. She had visited him there so often that it felt like a second home—and the other mechanics were like a second family, thanks to her dad's bragging. They knew almost everything about her.

"Hey, Nova!" one of the mechanics called out from underneath the Beetle he was repairing. "How'd it go with AP Chem?"

"Had a little trouble with the lab, but I aced the written!" she replied.

"Atta girl!" the mechanic said.

Another mechanic slid out from beneath a Toyota. "Finished with the prom decorations?" he asked.

"All done!" Nova said.

"Now all you need is a date!" the mechanic teased.

"Got one of those, too," Nova shot back. Then, in a quieter voice, she added, "Kind of."

A third mechanic turned away from the Ford he was fixing and rubbed his face, smearing grease on his cheek. "Yeah? Your old man gonna approve?" he asked with a playful twinkle in his eyes.

"Hi, Dad," Nova said. She followed Frank over to his workbench, which was almost overflowing with the report cards, prize ribbons, trophies, and school pictures that had been accumulating since Nova was in kindergarten. Frank carefully wiped the grease off his hands before giving his daughter a hug. "So who's the lucky guy? It's Brandon, right?"

Frank turned slightly and repeated—louder this time, so everyone in the garage could hear him— "Brandon. The one who applied pre-med to Princeton."

The rest of the mechanics nodded approvingly. They wanted only the best for Frank's little girl, too.

"Yeah, it's Brandon," Nova replied. She reached for a rag on the bench and used it to dab at some grease staining Frank's forehead. "But it's not exactly—"

"What?" Frank cut her off.

Nova hesitated. She had been utterly under-whelmed—disappointed, even—by Brandon's completely uninspired ask. But there was no reason her dad should be disappointed, too. The obvious pride that Frank took in all of her accomplishments only made Nova more determined to succeed at everything she did. She hadn't had to face his disappointment before.

And she wasn't about to start now.

"Nothing," Nova said brightly. "It's going to be great!"

"Of course it is," Frank said. "He's going with *you*!"

Nova smiled at her dad . . . and hoped he wouldn't notice the reluctance in her eyes.

After dinner, Nova went right to work tackling her to-do list. First on the agenda: setting up the brand-new web-cam she'd ordered . . . and teaching her dad how to use it. Though the family computer station was cluttered with cords and plastic bags and hundreds of packing peanuts, it didn't take long for Nova to hook up the webcam while her dad watched. She carefully adjusted it, tilting the camera slightly, and turned it on.

"See, there we are!" Nova said proudly as their faces appeared on the computer monitor. She moved behind her dad and reached forward to adjust the camera's position again. "You just make sure I'm online, too, and open the program on the desktop and choose me from the pull-down menu."

"No problem," Frank replied. "As long as you're sitting right here next to me to explain how to do it."

"Dad," Nova said. She could already tell what was coming.

"It's just . . . gonna be weird around here without you," Frank told her.

"That's why I'm showing you this," she said gently. "It'll be like I never left. Next fall, we can talk whenever you want."

Frank smiled at her. "Hmmm. Okay, how about . . . midnight . . . every night of the week?" he suggested.

"I don't know about that, Dad," Nova said with a laugh. "It's college. There'll be . . . stuff."

"Oh, yeah?" Frank asked, raising an eyebrow. "What kind of stuff? Haven't missed a curfew, ever. You gonna start then?"

"Oh, no, of course not, never," Nova teased him.

Frank laughed, but there was sadness in his eyes. "I'm so proud of you Nova. Getting that scholarship, going to Georgetown. That stuff is all I've ever wanted for you. And I know you're heading off to achieve great things."

He paused for a minute, clearly struggling with what was on his mind.

"It's the heading off part I'm just having a little trouble with," Frank finally finished.

There wasn't really anything Nova could say. All she could do was wrap her arms around her dad's broad shoulders and give him the biggest hug she could.

After a few more minutes of teaching Frank how to use the webcam, Nova escaped to her bedroom. It was already dark outside, and Nova knew that for her, a long night was just beginning. She unfurled the last Prom poster and gave it a long look. Then she taped it onto her wall and started unloading her backpack. A stack of books, a pile of notebooks, the enormous Prom binder, the unfinished floor plan, the blank ticket-selling schedule, another folder of stuff for student government—it was a lot. More than most people could handle.

Slowly, Nova pulled out the last item in her bag: the solitary Prom ticket Brandon had given her that afternoon. It looked so lonely all by itself. It looked so pathetic. Nova flipped open her laptop and tried to figure out where to begin. Suddenly, she felt so overwhelmed that making a decision was impossible. There was only one thing she could do.

Nova pushed aside the laptop, the books, and the papers . . . and especially the Prom ticket. She locked her door and closed the curtains. She turned off her phone and the lights. Finally alone at last, after the *longest* day, Nova flopped onto her bed, buried her face in a pillow, and screamed as loud as she could, again and again. She lay on the bed and listened to her own breathing for a few minutes.

Then she stood up, straightened her clothes, and undid all her secret-scream prep: lights on, curtains open, door unlocked, phone and laptop at the ready. Nova Prescott was back online and prepared to tackle the world . . . and then some.

That night, in the silent darkness that surrounded Brookside High after a busy school day, two people stood outside the storage shed: Tyler and Jordan. He reached for her hand as he stared into her eyes, which were shining in the moonlight. "I thought about what you said," Tyler said softly. "You do deserve an awesome Prom. So why wait?"

Tyler slid open the double doors to reveal two rows of pillar candles lighting a path into the center of the shed. He had spent hours that afternoon rearranging the Prom decorations that Nova and the rest of the committee had so carefully stored. The shed was just as cramped as before, but now running water trickled through the fountain, and all the star decorations glimmered, turning the shed into an utterly enchanting and romantic place.

Dozens of flickering candles didn't hurt, either.

"Wow," Jordan said as she took it all in.

"And what's Prom without a romantic dinner?" Tyler asked. He led Jordan around the fountain to a picnic blanket laid out with two cups of soda and two enormous burritos.

"You got Taco King?" Jordan exclaimed in delight.

"Vegetarian burrito, extra guac," Tyler replied. He'd made sure to get her all-time favorite takeout.

"You're the best!" she cried.

"So does that mean you'll go with me?" he asked. "To Prom?"

Jordan looked around the shed to cover her brief

moment of hesitation. "Yes," she said. "But Tyler, I want Prom night to be perfect. No drama. So if you're gonna be with me, then be with *me*."

Tyler looked shocked as he gestured at the enchantment all around them. "Come on. You think I'd do this for anyone but you?"

Tyler stared into Jordan's eyes with the right amount of intensity to convince her. She softened just a little, just enough, and he leaned in for a kiss. Their picnic dinner was as special and romantic as the early days when they were dating, back before things had gotten so complicated . . . and so weird. When Tyler looked at her like that, Jordan was almost able to forget all of her suspicions.

Almost.

A couple of hours later, just before curfew, Jordan and Tyler carefully went through the shed and blew out all the candles. They crept outside and slid the doors closed, never once imagining that there was one candle still lit, nestled way too close to a papier-mâché tree. It flickered in the gust of air from the closing doors.

But it didn't go out.

The orange flame ate away at the wick, growing stronger and stronger, until it was tall enough to reach the papier-mâché tree. The tree burst into flames, and seconds later, the fire began to lick at the centerpieces. They went up like torches, taking all of the stars with them, and soon the fountain was engulfed in flames. The fire spread like a plague, consuming all of the Prom Committee's hard work. In just minutes, the entire shed was ablaze—and there was no one who could do anything to stop it.

In her bedroom, with the laptop screen still glowing, Nova slept with her head on the desk, her unfinished work a poor excuse for a pillow. Despite all the pressure she was under, Nova slept peacefully, dreamlessly—the kind of rest that results from total exhaustion.

She had no idea of the nightmare that would be waiting for her at school in the morning.

CHAPTER

✦ ✮ SIX ✩ ✦

The buzz of a text and the ping of an IM woke Nova moments before her alarm went off. The message from Ali, sent to everyone on the Prom Committee, was short and scary.

DISASTER. GET 2 SCHOOL NOW.

Nova blinked her eyes sleepily and tried to wake up. As her head cleared, a rush of panic flooded through her. Nova didn't even waste a minute writing back—she just tossed all the books and papers into her bag and threw on the first clothes she grabbed out of her dresser.

Then Nova raced off to Brookside High as fast as she could.

It was clear to her that something was terribly wrong the moment she arrived. The air reeked from the stench of smoke. A red fire truck made official use of the emergency zone, and Nova nearly stumbled over a thick rubber hose as she followed the crowd around the back of the school to the place where the storage shed was.

Or—used to be.

The shed was gone; in its place stood a shell of steel beams that were blackened and warped from the fire's overwhelming heat. Glaring yellow DO NOT CROSS tape was roped around everything, keeping the students from getting too close to the scene of destruction. But Nova could tell, even from a distance, that the Prom decorations—what was left of them—were in tatters, charred and soaked and utterly ruined. Ali's expression was grim as she approached Nova.

But nothing could match the look of utter devastation on Nova's face.

The rest of the Prom Committee arrived soon after, and they stood together in a sad and shocked clump at the perimeter. With a quick glance around to make sure no adults were nearby, Nova slipped under the yellow tape to get a better look. One by one, Ali, Mei, Brandon, and Rolo followed her.

Rolo was the first to speak. "Whoa. It's like Apocalypse Prom."

Ali took a step closer to Nova. "Hey there . . ." she said cautiously.

"How are you . . . doing, Nova?" Brandon asked. He sounded afraid of the answer.

Nova didn't say a word. She just stared at the wreckage around them and moved closer to the fountain. The frame, at least, looked like it was still intact.

"At least the fountain survived," Rolo said hopefully.

Gingerly, Nova reached out a hand and touched the edge of the fountain. A huge piece immediately broke off and shattered on the ground.

"It's not supposed to do that, is it?" asked Rolo.

Everyone glared at him.

"Nova, what do we do now?" Mei dared to ask.

"Yeah, is Prom, like, cancelled?" Rolo said.

The rest of the committee held their breath. They were all secretly glad that Rolo had asked the question on everyone's mind. But still, Nova said nothing.

"We could postpone it 'til after graduation," Brandon suggested.

"Or just do it without decorations," Ali added.

The thought snapped Nova back to reality. "No," she said sharply. "No, no, and no. We rebuild."

The Prom Committee looked at her as if she'd lost her mind, but Nova didn't care.

"Guys. This is our prom," she pressed on. "If we give up, if we turn back now, then—"

"The terrorists have won?" cracked Rolo.

"People are *counting* on us," Nova continued loudly. "I'm not telling the entire senior class to return their dresses, cancel their dates, and forget the entire romantic prelude to the rest of their lives!"

"Nova, Prom's three weeks away," Mei pointed out.

"Then we work before school, after school, during school," Nova announced.

"Nova, I would but I can't," Mei replied. She looked miserable. "You know I have babysitting."

"Nova, I'm the lead in the spring musical," Ali said.

"Yeah, man," chorused Rolo. "This was already my hardest class this semester. I'm tapped out. I got nothing left."

Nova turned to Brandon, her last hope. Surely he wouldn't let a whole year's worth of work be for nothing.

"Brandon?" she asked.

But she already knew, from the look in his eyes, what his answer would be.

"Nova, AP tests are coming," he said. "I'm already behind."

Disappointment flashed across Nova's face, but it quickly gave way to indignation. "We worked so hard," she said angrily. "This isn't fair."

Nova spun around on her heel and stormed away.

"Nova! Where are you going?" Mei called after her.

Nova pushed through the crowd of people and marched straight up to Principal Dunnan, who was mobbed with kids and teachers and even firemen, all demanding his attention.

"Mr. Dunnan, we need to get these kids to class," one of the teachers said.

"Bill, the superintendent wants a full report before second period," Rhoda said anxiously.

"Sir, we need you over here," called one of the firemen.

But none of them were a match for Nova. "Mr. Dunnan," she began. "The Prom decorations are completely destroyed!"

Despite all the chaos, Nova's voice grabbed his attention.

"Nova. I know," he said, sighing heavily.

"This is *not* right. My committee worked very, very hard on those and now we don't have time to rebuild. What are we gonna do? What are *you* gonna do?" she demanded.

Mr. Dunnan didn't have any answers for her, but Nova wasn't about to go away. Suddenly, a new sound was heard above the crowd's chatter: the revving of a motorcycle. Mr. Dunnan's eyes narrowed as he wheeled around just in time to see Jesse pull up on his bike. Jesse shook his head as he removed his helmet and surveyed the destruction.

It was all too much for the principal.

"Mr. Dunnan?" Nova asked.

He marched over to Jesse, shaking his finger in the air. "Richter, get that pile of junk off school grounds. You can't ride that back here."

Jesse glanced around. There were at least a hundred students gawking at the mess. Why was he being singled out?

"Right, sorry," Jesse drawled sarcastically, "I wouldn't want any school property to get damaged."

"You think this is funny?" demanded Mr. Dunnan. "When people's hard work gets destroyed?"

"What was in there?" Jesse asked apathetically. "Just a bunch of dumb prom decorations, right?"

"Yeah. That's all," Principal Dunnan replied. "Just some dumb prom decorations that you're gonna rebuild."

"WHAT?" Jesse and Nova shouted simultaneously.

"Nova, you need help," Principal Dunnan reasoned, "and Richter, you clearly need something to keep you out of trouble for the next few weeks."

"Mr. Dunnan, really, I don't think—" Nova said at once.

"Oh, no, he's doing it," interrupted Mr. Dunnan. "Because if he doesn't, he won't graduate."

"What?" Jesse exploded. Beneath his anger, there was a very real worry that Mr. Dunnan would make good on the threat. And, as always, the unfairness—the enormous injustice of it all—tainted everything about this stupid school. "You can't do that! You can't keep me from graduating!"

"Ah, so there is something you care about, Richter," Principal Dunnan observed with a mean smile. "You wanna graduate? Then from now until Prom, you will spend every waking hour developing an appreciation for just how much work went into this project. We clear?"

Jesse was silent.

"Nothing funny to say?" asked Mr. Dunnan. "Didn't think so."

As Principal Dunnan hurried back to the other things demanding his attention, Nova stared at Jesse. Her eyes narrowed. Jesse was a far cry from her fellow enthusiastic Prom Committee members. But she didn't care how bad his attitude was. Nova knew that she needed all the help she could get, and she was ready to force Jesse to rebuild Prom with her.

One sparkly star at a time.

Brookside High was abuzz with talk about the fire for the rest of the day, but the news that Jesse Richter had been tasked with the rebuilding efforts spread like, well, wildfire. Despite all the drama, though, classes went on as usual—even if it was the most chaotic day of the school year so far.

As she hurried up the stairs to her next class, Simone noticed Lucas and Corey standing by their lockers. It would've been hard to miss them, actually—the two boys were wearing matching lacrosse helmets in the middle of the school day, and every senior who passed them took advantage of the opportunity to thump them on the head.

"Hi, guys," Simone called to them.

Corey and Lucas turned in opposite directions, knocking their helmets together loudly.

"What's with the helmets?" she asked.

"Varsity made us wear them," Lucas explained.

"It's . . . humiliating," added Corey.

"I think it's cute!" Simone smiled at them.

"Yeah, well. Wait 'til lunch," Lucas replied. "You'll change your mind if you see us try to eat pasta with them on."

Simone laughed, and the sound carried all the way down the hall to Tyler, who was messing around with some other guys from the varsity lacrosse team. When he glanced up and saw Simone smiling at Lucas, Tyler couldn't look away.

"I'll see you later, all right?" Simone asked.

"Sure," Lucas replied as he backed up, trying to look cool.

CLANG!

The sound of his helmet smashing into his locker reverberated throughout the entire second floor. Simone cringed, knowing it must have been a serious hit to make a noise like that.

"Are you okay?" she asked.

"Yeah, I'm fine," Lucas said, pointing at his head. "Helmet."

Simone laughed again as she went on her way. Tyler didn't stop watching her until she disappeared into a classroom. Despite all his promises to Jordan, in that moment all he could think about was how much he wanted to be with Simone.

During free period, Justin and Mei met up to hang out, just like they'd done every day since the start of freshman year. But today, someone else was sitting with them—Justin's friend Lloyd, who had been in a bad mood since the first Prom poster had appeared.

"Just ask someone," Mei said encouragingly. "It's really not that hard."

"Thank you, Oprah, for that nugget of wisdom," Lloyd said glumly.

"She's right," Justin pointed out.

"This from the guy who hasn't asked anyone out since middle school!" Lloyd complained. "You and Mei have been together forever, you're both going to Michigan, your whole lives are planned out. For the rest of us, yes, it is that hard."

"Dude, I just don't get how your *sister* convinced you

to ask someone," Justin said, shaking his head. "You've been ignoring my advice for years!"

As Lloyd shrugged, Mei grabbed her phone to check her e-mail. There was one new message waiting for her. Mei's eyes moved back and forth as she read it; then, without warning, she gasped, loud enough to get Justin's attention.

"What? What is it?" Justin asked, peering over her shoulder.

Mei seemed to shut down as she closed the e-mail. "Nothing," she said shortly. "Um. I just have to call my mom about something. Be right back."

Lloyd was oblivious as Mei jumped up and scurried away. "You know, you and I aren't that different," he said to Justin. "You're one Mei away from being *me*."

"Just ask someone already," Justin said impatiently as he watched Mei hurry off, anxiety radiating from her face. Something was bothering her, that much was obvious. But what? He didn't know.

And perhaps even more troubling, Justin could tell that whatever it was, whatever was going on—Mei didn't want to tell him.

* * *

That night, Lloyd couldn't stop thinking about what Justin had said. *Just ask someone already*. Lloyd was sure that those four little words were misleading, but he had to wonder . . . was it really that easy? Had Lloyd wasted the last four years when he could have been dating someone? Even his little sister seemed to think that he was making a big deal out of nothing—and it stung that a freshman girl had more guts than he did.

Just ask someone already.

Suddenly, Lloyd felt totally energized. He *would* ask someone. He would find some cute girl, maybe a girl who hadn't gotten to know a lot of people at Brookside during the last four years. A girl who might be a little shy, but who had an amazing personality once she opened up a little. A girl who was waiting for somebody else to make the first move.

A girl who was just like him.

Lloyd charged down the hall and knocked loudly on Tess's door.

"Enter," she called out in a funny voice.

"I'm gonna do it, Tess," he announced as he walked into her bedroom. "I'm gonna ask somebody to Prom tomorrow!"

"Go, Lloyd!" Tess cheered as she looked up from her history homework. "Who?"

For a moment, Lloyd's face was blank. Then he said, "Alice!"

Tess frowned a little. "Do I know her? Or maybe I should ask—does she know you?"

"She's in my gym class," Lloyd explained. "Of course she knows me. She's nice." Lloyd thought back to the time Alice had accidentally hit him in the back of the head with a basketball. It hadn't hurt—not that much, anyway—but it was obvious how terrible she felt. Her face had blushed bright red as she apologized about a dozen times, and she even looked like she wanted to cry. Best of all, Lloyd had cracked some dumb joke to make her feel better and she had smiled. Laughed a little, even.

Alice was definitely nice. And she was pretty cute, too.

"Well, good for you, Lloyd," Tess said as she turned back to her homework. "Now all you have to do is figure out the ask."

"The what?" Lloyd said, confused.

Tess glanced up again. "The ask. You know, whatever special thing you do to ask her," she replied. "It has to be *amazing*. Unforgettable. You can't just be all, 'Hey, wanna go to the Prom with me?' That would be such a fail."

"Yeah. Obviously," Lloyd said hesitantly. "I know that."

"Good luck," Tess said. "Let me know if you need any help."

"See you later," Lloyd said as he ducked out of Tess's room. But once he was back in the hallway, the confident smile faded from his face. Now he had to figure out an *ask*? Lloyd realized that he'd been right. Those four little words—just ask someone already—*were* completely misleading. Nothing was as simple as it seemed.

Lloyd roamed through the house, randomly walking from room to room as he waited for inspiration to hit. What made an ask unforgettable, anyway? Flowers? Balloons? Chocolate? That all seemed too generic . . . and too unoriginal. Lloyd knew that he had to think big. Something special. Something showy.

Inspiration hit when Lloyd spotted his mom's towering stack of magazines in the corner of the living room. Parenting magazines, gardening magazines, style magazines, news magazines . . . his mom subscribed to them all, but she never had time to read them. They just piled up in the living room until the stack got so tall that she chucked them all in the recycle bin. Lloyd knew that she would never miss a few of the older issues. He slipped a few of them out of the stack and grabbed a pair of scissors from the kitchen. It would only take a few cuts for Lloyd to have an unforgettable ask ready for tomorrow.

So unforgettable that it might just go down in history as one of Brookside's best Prom asks ever!

First thing in the morning, Lloyd and Tess snuck out early and left for school. She wouldn't quit asking for all the details about Lloyd's brilliant idea, but he kept his mouth shut—and the envelope of magazine clippings carefully hidden. He wanted *everyone* to be surprised . . . even his sister. Tess waited impatiently around the corner while Lloyd went to work on Alice's locker. When he finished, he took a long, hard look at his masterpiece.

It was perfect!

Colorful letters in all shapes and sizes spelled out a simple message on Alice's locker. It said:

Alice—I'Ve Been Watching You. Would you Go to Prom with Me???

Lloyd grinned at his handiwork, then moved away quickly as the first students started to arrive for school. He didn't want to give away the surprise too early. Lloyd positioned himself across the hall from Alice's locker and tried to look casual. He almost wished he'd brought one of those magazines to school, just so he could have something to do while he waited for Alice. Then again, he would have hated to miss the reaction of all the students filing in for the school day. At the sight of Alice's locker, everyone stopped and stared. Groups of girls started whispering to one another. Lloyd grinned again. He could feel himself becoming a legend already!

Then Lloyd noticed Alice and a friend approaching her locker, and his heart started to beat a little faster. Like everyone else who'd passed by, Alice stopped short. "What is that?" she exclaimed.

Lloyd wished that he could see her face. He had a feeling she was smiling . . . and was that a tremor in her voice? Was Alice about to cry tears of excitement?

"Oh my God!" Alice's friend replied.

"Who did this?" Alice said. Her voice rang down the hallway.

Lloyd took a step forward, ready to reveal himself

and take full credit. But then Alice spun around and Lloyd got a look at her face.

Alice was crying, all right. But they were definitely *not* tears of excitement. Alice looked angry—and terrified!

"I mean, what kind of sick twist would put creepy, serial killer letters on a person's locker?" she asked.

"Oh," Lloyd said to himself as Alice's friend tried to comfort her. Both girls started to look around suspiciously, trying to figure out who had vandalized her locker with the scary-looking letters. Lloyd knew that that was his cue to leave—fast. He hurried around the corner, where Tess was still waiting for him.

"How'd it go?" she asked eagerly.

But Lloyd just shook his head. "I was never here. You never saw me," he hissed. Then he power-walked down the hallway as fast as he could without running and looking even more suspicious. Lloyd knew one thing for certain.

He had to think of a new Prom date.

And he definitely had to come up with a new ask!

CHAPTER
✦ ✦ SEVEN ✦ ✦

Luckily for Lloyd, most people seemed to forget about the creepy message on Alice's locker by lunchtime. And by the time school got out, everyone else had moved on to more important things—like the lacrosse game.

Even though it was a varsity game, Lucas and Corey had to suit up, too. Weighed down with heavy pads over their jerseys, they could barely move, let alone transport the enormous jug of Gatorade. Grunting and panting, they struggled to lug the container across the field without spilling too much of the neon-colored drink on their uniforms.

"You have to ask her out!" Corey insisted as he paused to get a better grip.

"I don't know . . ." Lucas said, glancing around nervously. A ton of students had gathered for the game, but they all seemed to be out of earshot. He definitely didn't want anyone besides Corey to suspect how he felt about Simone.

"You're killing me!" groaned Corey.

From the middle of the field, where the varsity players were warming up, Tyler spotted Lucas and Corey dragging the Gatorade container. Then he remembered the way Simone had been laughing and hanging out with the little twerps. An idea started to form in his mind. Tyler jogged away from the team and grinned at the boys as he leaned down and easily lifted the gallons of Gatorade.

"There you go, fellas," Tyler said over his shoulder as he carried the beverage over to the bench.

"We totally had that," Corey said under his breath.

Tyler paid no attention to him. "Hey, Lucas," he continued. "You're looking good out there, bro."

"Really?" Lucas asked in surprise.

"He *is*?" Corey asked, sounding even more shocked than Lucas.

"You've got real varsity potential," Tyler said, nodding his head.

"He *does*?" Corey said.

From under his helmet, Lucas shot Corey a look that made him scuttle away, mumbling to himself.

"Wow, thanks, Tyler," Lucas said. "I don't know what to say."

"I'm having a team barbecue on Thursday. You should swing by," said the upperclassman.

"Really?" Lucas repeated. It was surprising enough that Tyler had even noticed him. But an invitation? To a varsity barbecue? That was earth-shattering.

"Totally casual. Bring a friend if you want," Tyler added.

"Corey?" asked Lucas.

Tyler frowned. "I was thinking more like a *girl*, Lucas."

"Oh. Right," Lucas said awkwardly.

"You do know some of those, don't you?" Tyler teased him.

"Oh, yeah. Of course. Tons," Lucas replied, hoping that he sounded convincing.

Thweeeeeeeeeeeeeeeeeeeet!

The coach's whistle blasted: it was almost time for

the game to begin. Tyler turned back to the field, wink-ing at Lucas as he jogged past him. "See you there, bro!" he called.

Still shocked, Lucas sat down next to the Gatorade jug as his thoughts raced wildly. A barbecue at Tyler's house . . . with the varsity team . . . and he was supposed to bring a *girl*?

There was only one person Lucas could imagine asking, and the thought was enough to make his hands start sweating and his face grow hot. Asking Simone out would've been hard enough.

But taking her to a place where the entire varsity team would be watching?

That sounded more like torture than a date.

Far away from the sun-drenched athletic field, Nova found herself in the old basement art room that smelled like mildew and poster paint. The overhead fluorescent lights buzzed loudly, their sickly greenish light giving her a headache. As she lugged in the few decorations that had been salvaged from the shed, her mood got worse by the minute. She stopped to catch her breath by the twisted, blackened shell of the burned-up fountain that she had dragged into the center of the room. It looked pathetic.

Nova spun around to bring in the next batch of supplies when she suddenly noticed Jesse standing in the doorway, his arms full of the supplies she needed. Her eyes darkened as she stared at him in annoyance.

For a moment, neither one spoke. At last, Nova broke the silence. "Right there's fine," she said shortly, pointing at the floor.

Without speaking, Jesse leaned down to place all the supplies in a neat pile. Nova couldn't help noticing his arm muscles under his cotton T-shirt. He was really built. Just as quickly, she caught herself and tried to look away—but not before she saw the way he pushed his dark hair out of his face.

Their eyes met, and Jesse waited silently for the next instruction.

Nova glanced around the cluttered art room. Ever since the brand-new bright and breezy art room had been built, this pit in the basement didn't get much use. It looked like a graveyard for abandoned art projects, some of them created by students who had graduated years ago. But at this point in the school year, it was about the only place left that Nova could use as Prom decoration headquarters—especially now that the shed was gone.

Her gaze stopped at a dozen enormous reams of fabric leaning precariously against one wall. "You know, why don't you move all of that stuff over there," she suggested, pointing to the opposite wall. "Think you can do that without getting into trouble?"

Jesse still didn't speak. One by one, he began to move the heavy bolts across the room. Meanwhile, Nova started taking inventory of the supplies that had been left in the art room long ago. With her head buried in a giant crate, she didn't notice Jesse peel off his T-shirt to reveal a tight-fitting tank undershirt. When she did look up, Nova stumbled right into a sealed tub of plaster.

"Ow!" she exclaimed.

"Problem?" Jesse asked without looking up.

"No," Nova said through clenched teeth. "I'm just . . . taking inventory of this bucket."

"That would be 'one,'" he replied.

Nova focused on slowing her beating heart and glared at him as she reached down to pick up the bucket. Why would she feel flustered around Jesse? She liked

Brandon. Smart, dependable, level-headed Brandon. Jesse was nothing but a loser.

"You want help with that?" Jesse said when he noticed Nova struggling with the heavy bucket.

"Oh, yes, maybe you could give it a long, brooding stare until it carries itself across the room," she said. "No thanks."

"You sure you don't want help?" he asked again. "Because moving this—" he gestured at the fabric "—seems kind of pointless and stupid."

"Well, you'd be the authority on pointless and stupid," Nova snapped. Defiantly, she reached for the bucket again, hoisted it into the air—and lost her balance. She sprung up again immediately, ignoring Jesse's enjoyment. Nova was determined to move that bucket by herself if it was the only thing she got done that day.

"Wait," Jesse said as he rushed to her side. "Nova, wait. Hold on. I just want to say one thing."

From the tone of Jesse's voice, Nova suspected that he was about to apologize. She held her head high and waited.

He stood very close to her, staring at her with an unfamiliar intensity. As their eyes locked, he leaned in even closer.

"Lift from the legs," he whispered.

Nova jerked away, so angry she was shaking. She took a quiet, deep breath to get control of her temper. She wasn't about to let a loser like Jesse Richter see how much he had affected her.

No matter what.

But at home that night, with her mom and dad listening sympathetically, Nova let it all out. "He's a *menace*," she ranted. "A rude, arrogant menace with no sense of personal space. And he was late. I don't know if Dunnan's punishing him or me."

"What's his name?" Frank asked angrily. "Jesse Richter? The punk who stocks shelves at the market?"

"I think he works there." Nova shrugged. Not that she cared.

"Knew his father," declared Frank. "Apple didn't fall far from the tree."

"He's a teenager, Frank," Kitty, Nova's mom, said gently.

"Dunnan thinks this whole thing is some kind of character-building exercise or something," Nova explained, rolling her eyes. "Why can't he just make him pick up trash off the side of the road like all the other delinquents?"

"Is there any chance Jesse might actually help you?" Kitty said, loud enough that both Nova and Frank turned to look at her.

"Kitty, he's a punk," Frank said. "He's not going to become an upright citizen all of a sudden."

"I didn't say that," Kitty replied. "I'm just saying, it seems like you could use the help, Nova. Three weeks isn't a lot of time."

"Help, sure," Nova admitted. "But he's a . . ."

"A walking misdemeanor," Frank said, winking at his daughter.

"Right!" Nova exclaimed. "Thank you!"

Kitty just shook her head. She knew better than to interfere with the bond between Frank and Nova.

"I'm a tough guy, I drive a motorcycle, I can lift heavy stuff, I have long hair," Nova mocked Jesse ruthlessly.

The corners of Kitty's lips twitched into the tiniest smile as she watched Nova continue ranting. In her experience, there was only one kind of explanation for that kind of passionate rage.

And it had nothing to do with real anger.

When the doorbell rang, Kitty excused herself to answer it. But Nova just couldn't stop. "You should see this guy, Dad," she continued. "It's like he enjoys watching me suffer."

"If this kid gives you any more problems, you come to me," Frank said firmly.

Nova grinned at him. What would she do without her dad?

"Nova! It's for you," Kitty called from the front hall.

Nova raised her eyebrows in surprise; she wasn't expecting anyone. She hurried into the living room, where she found Brandon waiting for her, looking more excited than she'd ever seen him.

"Hi, Brandon," she began. "What are you—"

"I got into Princeton!" he exclaimed.

"That's amazing! Congratulations!" she shrieked.

In the kitchen, Kitty and Frank listened attentively to every word. As Frank started a victory dance, Kitty rolled her eyes.

"That's not all," Brandon continued proudly. "I'm a finalist for the Dean's Scholarship."

Nova's eyes lit up. "Brandon, that's amazing!" she cried as she gave him a hug.

"Thanks," he replied. "I knew you'd understand."

"The Dean's Scholarship?" Nova said, laughing. "Who wouldn't understand? That's awesome!"

"No," Brandon said, shaking his head. "The interview for the scholarship is the same weekend as Prom."

It took a moment for Nova to fully understand what he meant. Her face started to fall before she checked herself. "Oh," was all she could say.

"I hate to leave you hanging," he said apologetically.

Nova forced a smile. "No, I completely get it," she said quickly, surprised by how normal her voice could be when she felt like she was dying inside.

"Really?" Brandon asked hopefully.

"Really," Nova insisted, telling herself to smile bigger, to smile harder, to sound like she meant it. "Don't give it another thought. I mean, Princeton! Go, Tigers!"

"You're the greatest," said Brandon.

"I try," she replied, hoping to sound fun and playful.

It wouldn't do any good for Brandon to know how crushed she was.

Now if only Nova could keep her real feelings hidden until he left. Mentally, she was already reworking her to-do list. Nova knew that she needed to clear her schedule for a good, long cry. After the decorations had been destroyed, Nova had thought nothing else could go wrong.

But being stranded without a date . . . less than three weeks before Prom . . . by the guy she'd been falling for all spring?

That was a disaster even Nova was unprepared to face.

CHAPTER
EIGHT

In science lab the next day, Lucas watched the door anxiously, waiting for Simone to appear.

Corey hovered nearby, still marveling at the invitation Lucas had snagged. "Tyler Barso's barbecue," he repeated yet again, shaking his head in disbelief.

"Is this my Hendrix moment?" Lucas asked, never taking his eyes off the doorway.

Just then, Simone and her friends walked into the classroom. As the girls stashed their bags and books in the back of the lab, Corey snapped to attention. "*That* could be your Hendrix moment," he said, nodding toward Simone.

Lucas swallowed as he tried to psych himself up.

"But first," Corey said, grabbing Lucas's shoulder and turning him around. "Fly check."

Lucas subtly reached down and confirmed that his pants were zipped up. (Thankfully!)

"Pit check," Corey advised, and Lucas leaned over to his armpits. He sniffed heavily, but didn't smell anything except a whiff of his antiperspirant, which was definitely working overtime. (Thankfully!)

"Now, breathe on me," Corey finished.

Lucas made a face. "What? Why?"

"Breath check," explained Corey. "The most crucial of all. You want to ask her out with butt mouth? Come on, hit me."

Lucas hesitated before he reluctantly leaned close to Corey's face. In one fast puff, he exhaled.

Corey shook his head. "I didn't get anything," he said. "Hit me again."

"Corey," Lucas groaned.

"I just had a cough drop, my olfactory nerves are compromised!" Corey explained. But when Lucas didn't make a move, Corey practically stuck his nose in Lucas's mouth and inhaled deeply.

"What are you guys doing?"

At the sound of Simone's voice, Corey and Lucas leaped apart, mortified. "Molecular experiment! Condensation!" Corey babbled. "I gotta go." He slunk off to his own lab station, blushing bright red—even his ears.

"He's . . . weird," Lucas said lamely.

"Yeah," Simone agreed. She turned to the lab table and started arranging the beakers and crucibles.

For just a moment, Lucas watched her pretty hands hover over the lab equipment; then his eyes moved to her gorgeous hair, shining in the sunlight that streamed through the large windows. He took a deep breath.

It was now or never.

"So, um, I'm glad you're here," he began. "I mean, I knew you'd be here. This *is* our class. Not that you never miss class. I mean, you don't miss a lot of class or anything. You have excellent attendance as far as I can tell."

"I try," Simone replied. She smiled at him over her shoulder and he felt, for a moment, that he could do this—he could ask her out—without acting like a total idiot.

"There's a lacrosse team barbecue on Thursday and I was wondering if you wanted to go with me?" Lucas blurted out. "I mean, unless you have a . . . lacrosse issue. Which some people do. Sometimes."

The seven seconds before Simone answered were an agony for Lucas. Then her broad, warm smile put him at ease.

"That sounds like fun," she said. After that miserable scene with Tyler in the janitor's closet, a relaxed barbecue with a cute guy sounded like exactly what she needed.

Lucas couldn't hide his surprise—or his relief. "Really?" he asked.

"Sure," Simone said. "I love a good barbecue."

As she turned back to preparing the lab station, Lucas glanced over his shoulder at Corey, who was watching from a few tables behind them. He mouthed, "She loves barbecues!"

Corey responded in the only way he knew—with an extreme air-guitar solo.

Was there any other way to celebrate his best friend's Hendrix moment?

That day, Nova spent every free minute—midmorning break, lunch, study hall—in the musty old art room. She returned there right after school, too.

Not much about her time at Brookside had intimidated her. But the thought of rebuilding all the Prom decorations in less than three weeks was enough to make her break out in a cold sweat . . . especially, Nova knew, since she couldn't count on help from anyone else. It was already after three o'clock and Jesse hadn't even bothered to show up.

When he finally walked into the art room, she shot him a look that would have scared away a pit bull. "We start every day at three," she said, not wasting time on pleasantries like "Hey" or "How's it going?"

"Dude, relax," Jesse replied as he turned around a chair and sat on it backwards. "It's three-fifteen."

"Okay, I'm not a 'dude,'" Nova snapped. "And I know what time it is. You're late."

"You know, in case you hadn't noticed, I'm the only one here," Jesse said. "Would you rather me be here late, or not at all?"

"Uh, not at all," Nova said. "Was I not giving off that vibe? 'Cause I'll try harder." She turned her attention back to the broken fountain, which she'd already started to redecorate. Now it was time to hook it up to see if it would still work.

"What's that supposed to be?" Jesse asked.

"A celestial fountain," Nova said shortly.

"Well, it's gonna leak all over the *celestial* floor unless you fix the diverter on the intake valve," Jesse pointed out.

"I know that," Nova lied. But as Jesse came over to take a closer look at the tubes snaking out of the fountain, she felt a sudden and surprising burst of relief. Jesse definitely knew what was wrong—and he sounded like he might know how to fix it.

Maybe he wouldn't be so useless, after all . . . if she couldn't figure it out on her own, of course.

As Mei and Justin walked home from school that day, as they had every day for the past five years, Justin couldn't stop talking about Prom. Mei was only half-listening, nodding and saying "Yeah" and "Uh-huh," at all the right times. It was a pretty good cover, but Justin could tell there was something else on her mind. So he ramped up the Prom talk even more, hoping she'd get as excited as he was.

What Justin didn't know was that Prom had turned into Mei's least favorite subject—ever since the e-mail she'd gotten in the quad. And that wasn't the only secret she was keeping from him. She had some big decisions to make. Decisions she needed to make on her own, without anyone else's input.

Not even Justin's.

"This is gonna be so awesome!" Justin exclaimed, still prattling on about Prom. "Mark and I booked the limo. He's taking Izzy, of course. Now, about the tux, are you thinking traditional black, or—"

Mei suddenly snapped out of her daze. "Mark and Isabelle?" she asked.

"Yeah. Is that cool?" Justin replied.

"Yeah. It's fine," she said. But her face and her tone told Justin she didn't mean that at all.

"It doesn't sound fine," he said carefully.

"I said it's fine," Mei repeated.

Justin stopped walking. "Mei, if something's wrong . . ." he began.

"Why are you hounding me?" she demanded.

"What?" Justin asked in surprise. "I'm not."

"It's just, Mark and Isabelle are kind of your friends . . ." Mei said, looking away from Justin, far down the street.

"What?" Justin said again.

"Do I get any say in this at all?" Mei continued. She still wouldn't meet his eye.

"Yes, of course you do," Justin replied. He was confused.

"How many other things have you figured out?"

"Nothing. I haven't—"

"You haven't figured *anything* out?" Mei cut him off.

"No, that's not what I meant!" Justin said. "Look, I had no idea you felt this way. I'll cancel with them. It can be just us. Forget I ever said anything."

In silence, they started walking again. Justin, struggling to put words to the feeling gnawing at his heart finally gave up and just reached for her hand, hoping that his touch would say what he could not.

Mei listlessly took his hand as she stared off at the skyline. From here, it seemed as distant and small as she felt.

A few miles away, on an overpass above a busy highway, Lloyd put his latest plan into effect. He'd stayed up half the night painting a message on an old sheet, making sure that the letters were large and neat and that the message itself was completely clear . . . with absolutely no room for mistaken interpretations. Lloyd's face screwed into a grimace of concentration as he unfurled the enormous sheet directly over the northbound lanes, and secured it with a thick roll of duct tape.

Lloyd checked his watch. It hadn't been too tough for Tess to find out that every day, shortly after 4:30, Jen drove under this overpass on her way home from gymnastics. The clock was ticking. Lloyd decided to be on the safe side and unveil the sign a little early. The sheet fell over the concrete guardrail with a loud *whoosh*.

Suddenly, Lloyd saw Jen's car approaching! There was no way she could miss his seven-foot sign . . . and there was no way she would think it was anything but an adorable, over-the-top public ask. If this sign didn't get him noticed, Lloyd knew that nothing would.

Then the unthinkable happened.

An eighteen-wheeler barreled down the southbound lane, barely clearing the overpass as it ripped down Lloyd's sign!

"Oh, no. No, no!" Lloyd moaned.

The banner fluttered away on the truck as it zoomed off, just moments before Jen drove by. She missed the banner, missed the ask, even missed Lloyd standing on the overpass, a look of despair on his face. Once again, Lloyd's ask had been ruined. He was running out of ideas.

And he was running out of time.

The next day at lunch, Lloyd was still in a terrible mood. Senior year had been going along just fine until prom fever had hit Brookside—but now that Lloyd had caught it, Prom was all he could think about.

"Prom," Lloyd said in despair the next day at lunch as he and Justin drowned their sorrows in chocolate milk—or tried to.

"Prom," echoed Justin, sounding just as frustrated as Lloyd. "Women!"

"Women," Lloyd repeated, shaking his head miserably.

After dinner that night, Nova returned to the art room to work on the fountain again. All by herself, she fumbled with the switch and crossed her fingers for luck. She could hear the rush of water through the tubes, and suddenly—victory! Water streamed out of the fountain's jets in perfect arches. The celestial fountain was absolutely stunning. Nova could already tell that in twenty years, when everybody came back for a Brookside Class of 2011 reunion, they would still be talking about it.

Then a sudden grinding sound, like a fork caught in a garbage disposal, shattered her fantasy. "Oh, no," Nova begged. "Please don't do this . . ."

But it was too late. Water was spilling everywhere, pooling under the fountain and soaking the decorations Nova had just added to it.

"And . . . it's leaking," came a voice from the doorway.

Nova sighed. She didn't even have to turn around to know that Jesse was standing there, smirking. "Yeah. You happy?"

Jesse shrugged. "Amused," he replied.

At least he was honest about it.

With long, even strides Jesse crossed the room and knelt next to Nova. He unplugged the fountain and pulled out its motor. Nova stared at him curiously, noticing the intense look of concentration on his face.

"You act all tough, but I know you," she said as a small grin flitted across her lips. "You're the guy who cried when the class hamster died in third grade."

"Yeah, well, *Heddy* didn't make me build a cosmic canopy," he shot back.

"You remember her name!" Nova crowed. "You just need a hamster to love, don't you?"

"These motors can be tricky," Jesse spoke over her.

Nova sighed again as he pulled the casing off the motor and started fiddling with the colored wires inside it. "This is a disaster," she groaned.

"A hurricane is a disaster," Jesse corrected Nova. "Smallpox, locusts, those are disasters. This is just a fountain. And it's just Prom."

"*Just* Prom?" Nova asked incredulously.

"Yeah," Jesse said, amused by the look of absolute disbelief that crossed Nova's pretty face. "Lame DJ. Poofy dresses. Balloons. Not worth getting that worked up over."

"I forgot, school functions conflict with your 'thinking I'm better than everyone' time," Nova replied. "For the rest of us, Prom happens to be fun."

Jesse shook his head. "Not for the guys," he said. "You gotta buy the dinner, you gotta get the little flower thing. . . ."

"Don't pretend you don't know what it's called."

"And then there's the tuxedo—the ultimate symbol of conformity that a bunch of other guys have already sweated in."

"Oh, right." Nova laughed. "Whereas you opt for the leather jacket and motorcycle—the clichéd symbol of nonconformity."

"At least I don't wear it posing in front of some lame backdrop," Jesse shot back.

"People save those pictures forever," Nova replied.

"In a box in their attic."

"Everyone remembers their prom," she insisted.

"Everyone remembers the stomach flu," cracked Jesse.

"A lot of people worked really hard," Nova said, and she sounded quieter than before.

"Just to have it all burn down," Jesse said, staring at the motor in his hands.

Nova didn't respond.

Jesse glanced up and noticed the unusual shine in Nova's eyes. He cleared his throat. "Look, I'm sorry. Prom is obviously very important to you. I just don't get it, all this for one night." Jesse flung out his arm, gesturing at the dripping fountain, the half-finished decorations, the spilled glitter and scraps of shiny foil all over the floor.

"Yeah," Nova admitted. "It's just one night, just a dance. But it's the *last* night. The *last* dance. And for that one night, there's nothing behind us and nothing ahead, just all of us in this one perfect moment."

Nova took a deep breath to steady herself. She forced herself not to cry, and when she spoke again, her voice was even and strong. "And I want to be a part of that."

Jesse glanced back down at the motor, and quicker than he realized, Nova was on her feet and out the door.

He waited for five minutes, ten, then twenty. But Nova didn't come back.

As the minutes passed, a familiar scowl settled over Jesse's face. He meant what he'd said to Nova, every word of it: Prom was a complete and total waste of time.

So why was he waiting around, hoping she would come back?

And why did he feel so lousy now that she had left?

CHAPTER
NINE

For Ali, study hall was no fun anymore—not since Nova had started spending every minute of her day holed up in the old art room—so she decided to get some computer time in the library instead. To her delight, she spotted a free computer right next to Rolo. Ali's eyes glinted wickedly. This seemed like a perfect time to find out all about his "girlfriend," the so-called Athena from Canada.

"Hey, Rolo," Ali said brightly as she plunked down on a chair next to him. "Can I see Athena's profile?"

"She doesn't have one," Rolo replied, glancing at Ali out of the corner of his eye.

"Really?" Ali asked, faking surprise. "No profile? Athena stays off the grid?"

"Actually, she had to take her page down because she got grounded," Rolo explained as he stared at the computer screen.

"So she's dangerous," Ali replied. "What's she in for?"

"She was out clubbing 'til late."

Ali's whole face lit up. "Athena likes to get up in the club, huh?" she asked gleefully.

"Yeah," Rolo said, nodding his head as his eyes grew even wider than usual. "Big time."

Ali shifted in her chair and leaned down, pretending to turn on the computer. It was a good cover—angled away from Rolo so he couldn't see how hard she was fighting back the laughter.

Late that afternoon, Corey cruised down the street in his mom's car, driving at least fifteen miles under the speed limit. In the backseat, Lucas cleared his throat nervously. "It should be this next block," he spoke up as he snuck a glance at Simone, sitting across from him. She noticed and smiled back.

"Thanks for driving, Corey," Simone said.

"Sure thing," Corey replied, his eyes glued to the road. "I'm a driver. I can drive."

"As long as it's daylight hours and with adult supervision," Corey's mom spoke up from the front seat. "Now slow down."

Corey made a face, but he did slow down even more. "What is that sound?" he asked loudly. "I could swear it's my mom nagging me, but that's impossible since she promised to be quiet during this car ride."

"Use your signal," his mom replied.

The *click-click-click* of the turn signal was the only sound as Corey slowly pulled up in front of Tyler Barso's house. Simone followed Lucas out of the car, then leaned down to the window. "Aren't you coming, Corey?" she asked.

"Oh, only Lucas was invited," Corey's mom told her.

"Silence!" Corey ordered.

"But it's a team barbecue," Simone said, frowning.

"Oh, yeah, it is, but it's . . ." Lucas's voice trailed off as the front door swung open, revealing Tyler in the doorway. Simone noticed him at once. She froze as she put it all together.

"Varsity," Lucas finished.

"Oh. That explains it," Simone replied, trying to

play it cool. "Um, guess we should go in. Thanks again, Corey."

"No problem," Corey said. "You kids have fun . . . without me . . . And if you need a ride home in"— Corey peered out the windshield, trying to figure out the position of the setting sun—"seventy-five minutes or so, call me."

Corey watched Lucas and Simone walk up to the front door with just a hint of envy in his eyes. Then, checking the rearview mirror, and glancing behind him to look for oncoming traffic, he eased his mom's car into the street, and drove away . . . slowly.

"Hey, Lucas!" Tyler called from the porch. "You made it!"

"Hey, Tyler," Lucas replied. "This is Simone."

"We've met," Simone said coolly.

"Oh, really?" Lucas asked her.

"Doesn't everyone know Tyler Barso?" she replied.

Neither Tyler nor Lucas knew what to say to that. Then Tyler flashed his winning smile at Simone. "Come on in," he said as he held open the door.

Lucas and Simone followed Tyler through the house to the backyard, which was crowded with seniors. They were the only two underclassmen at the barbecue.

The smoky smell of the grill hung heavily in the air, making Lucas realize how hungry he was. He noticed a long table full of chips, brownies, burgers, and hot dogs, and wondered when he could head over there to fix up a plate.

Simone, however, had lost her appetite the moment she saw Tyler Barso. And when she noticed that they were approaching a group of senior girls—including Jordan—Simone knew that she had to get away. She leaned close to Lucas. "Um, I'll be right back, okay," she whispered, hurrying off before he could respond.

"Hey, guys, this is Lucas," Tyler said smoothly as he introduced Lucas to the girls. "He's on the team."

"Oh yeah? What position are you?" Jordan asked.

"Seated. Usually," Lucas replied.

Miraculously, all the seniors laughed. Lucas couldn't believe it. Was he actually . . . funny?

As the girls focused on Lucas, Tyler spotted his chance—and took it. Without a word, he slipped away, and almost nobody noticed.

Except for Jordan.

Her eyes narrowed as she watched Tyler amble over to the cooler, where Simone was sipping a soda.

"Hi," he said as he stood next to her.

"Don't talk to me," Simone replied, her mouth thin and tight.

"C'mon. Don't play it like that," Tyler said. "I'm glad you're here. I miss you."

"I had no idea this was your party," Simone said coldly. She refused to look at him.

Tyler raised an eyebrow. "You sure about that?" he asked. "There wasn't a teeny, tiny part of you that wanted to see me, too?"

Simone couldn't bear to admit that he might be right. So she turned and walked away, pushing right through the crowd of seniors to find Lucas.

"Hey," she said breathlessly.

In an instant, he was completely focused on her.

"Hey!" Lucas replied. "What's up? Where did you go?"

"Just to get a drink," she said vaguely. "Do you, uh, want to get out of here?"

"You want to leave?" Lucas asked. "Is everything okay?"

"Yeah, sure." Simone shrugged, trying to sound casual. "I'm just not really into this party scene right now."

Lucas nodded. "I get that," he replied. "Come on.

Let's grab some food and see if we can find a quieter place to hang out. Cool?"

Simone actually smiled—for the first time since she'd seen Tyler. "Cool," she said. "Let's do it."

Over at the food table, Simone and Lucas fixed up some burgers and filled their plates with sides. Then, with a shy smile, Lucas led her over to a corner of the yard, where Tyler's old tree house was perched in a sturdy oak. They slipped around the back of the trunk to a hidden ladder, and no one noticed them sneak up into the tree house.

One look inside the tree house told Lucas and Simone that Tyler still used it, even though he was about to graduate from high school. But it was clear that Tyler had moved beyond the old games of pirates and cowboys that he probably played up here; now the tree house was actually a pretty cool hangout, with oversize all-weather beanbag chairs and posters of athletes and rock bands all over the walls. There was even a guitar tucked into a corner.

Up in the tree house, Simone and Lucas could still hear all the noise from the party below, but there was something far more appealing about hiding out among the leafy branches as the soft light of dusk spilled through the open windows. Simone started to relax a little as she and Lucas ate their burgers, and she realized how amazing it was to be up here, just with him, away from everyone else at the party . . . especially Tyler.

When a frantically upbeat pop song started playing on the stereo system in Tyler's backyard, Simone made a face. "Oh, no, not this song!" she groaned.

Lucas's eyes brightened. "You . . . hate this song, too?" he asked hopefully.

"Ugh, it has, like, eight words, and two of them are 'party,'" Simone complained.

"If this were my world, Corey and I would have veto power over all music released into the airwaves!" Lucas said, his voice full of excitement.

"Just you guys?" Simone teased him.

Lucas almost started to blush. "Well, you, too," he corrected himself. "If you wanted."

"Thanks," Simone said with a grin. She reached behind him and grabbed the guitar. "So, do you walk the walk, or just talk the talk?"

"You mean, do I play?" Lucas asked ruefully. "Um, no."

"Wanna learn?"

Lucas stared at her. "Um . . ."

"Here," Simone said, placing the guitar in his arms. "Now you put your hand like this . . ." Simone took Lucas's hand in hers, and his breath caught in his throat at the softness of her skin, the lightness of her touch. Her face was full of concentration as she placed his hands on the neck of the guitar, but Lucas couldn't take his eyes off her.

"No . . . almost . . . okay!" Simone said at last, smiling triumphantly. "That's a C."

"C," Lucas repeated softly.

"Yeah. But you have to strum," Simone said, with nothing but sweetness in her voice.

"Ah," Lucas said, laughing nervously. He strummed the guitar, but the sound it made was terrible.

Simone leaned forward to adjust his hands. Her hair fell over her eyes; as she blew it out of her face, her lower lip made the most adorable pout.

Lucas had spent most of the semester thinking about how much he liked Simone.

But that was nothing compared to how he was feeling about her right now.

"Okay," Simone said, totally oblivious to how hard

Lucas was falling for her. "Try now."

Lucas tried to focus as he strummed the guitar. This time, to his complete and total shock, it didn't sound that terrible.

It actually sounded pretty good!

"There you go!" Simone exclaimed. "You'll be a rock god in no time!"

Her excitement was infectious, and before he'd thought it through, Lucas blurted out, "Do you have a boyfriend?"

The second after he spoke, Lucas wished he could take it back. It was impossible to miss the cloud that fell over Simone's pretty face.

"Sorry," he said in a rush. "I mean, it's not my business." He strummed the guitar again and sang out, "C."

"No, it's okay," Simone said, recovering quickly. "There was somebody, but it turned out he wasn't really . . . available."

"Oh," Lucas said awkwardly. "Sorry."

Simone smiled at him, and the cloud disappeared as quickly as it had arrived. "It's okay," she replied firmly. "I'm over it."

Once again, she reached out to adjust Lucas's hands on the guitar. Lucas looked at the sky through the slats in the tree-house roof, where the first stars were just beginning to appear, and mouthed a silent *Yes*!

Lucas's elation hadn't faded at all by the next morning, when he and Corey met up at their lockers before homeroom. He was so caught up in telling Corey about every moment of his afternoon with Simone that he didn't even notice the scowl on Corey's face.

"She doesn't have a boyfriend!" Lucas reported gleefully. "She told me. And she plays guitar!"

"Lucas," Corey began.

"I mean, it's just like you said . . ." Lucas continued.

"You don't listen to what I say," his friend muttered.

". . . she's into me," Lucas went on. "Right? Which is why I'm going to ask her to study as soon as I see her."

"*Hey*," Corey said, loud enough that Lucas finally paid attention to him. "Did you forget what day it is?"

Lucas looked confused. "Friday?" he guessed.

"Friday. Yes," Corey said, on the verge of losing his patience. "Which we've established and designated as Stick Hippo T-Shirt Day. Where's yours?"

Corey faced Lucas, proudly displaying their favorite band's iconic T-shirt—the one with a stick figure-style animal with a bulging hippo's head.

"I . . . guess I forgot," Lucas said lamely.

"I have an extra," Corey said with a sigh. "For emergencies."

As Corey turned around to rummage in his locker, Lucas spotted Tyler moving down the hall, surrounded—as always—by a group of friends from the team.

"Tyler!" Lucas yelled, waving wildly. "Great party, bro!"

Tyler glanced over and gave Lucas a nod. "You're the man, Luke," he called back.

Lucas could barely contain his grin. Corey, still searching through his locker, just shook his head in disgust. *Luke?* Who was Luke? What had happened to his best friend?

Things only got worse during lab class. As soon as they got to the door, Lucas broke away from Corey and went straight to Simone, with a whole new confidence that Corey had never seen before in his buddy.

"Hey, Simone," Lucas said. "Listen, if you want to study for the chemistry test after school . . ."

"I'd love to," she interrupted him. "I really need it!"

"How about we meet in the library?" Lucas suggested.

"Perfect," Simone said, smiling in that way that always gave Lucas such a thrill. "I'll be there."

Behind him, Corey reached out and tapped Lucas on the shoulder. "I thought *we* were gonna study," he said.

"Dude. I'm sealing the deal," Lucas whispered.

"Right. Yeah. Totally," Corey said, nodding. "I'll study alone . . . much better. I'll be good."

But Lucas had already turned back to Simone.

It almost seemed like he didn't care one way or the other. And whether or not that was the message Lucas meant to send, it was the one that Corey got . . . loud and clear.

★ ♥ ✦ TEN ☆ ♥ ★

"She's alone. Go for it," Tess whispered.

Lloyd peered around Tess at Kristen, who had just arrived at her locker. As he watched Kristen send a text message, Lloyd gulped nervously. "What do I say?" he asked.

Tess sighed. "Just pretend you're a normal person," she replied, giving him a little push.

Lloyd took a deep breath as he got ready to pump himself up. After his last two disastrous attempts, the dream of the "big ask" was over. Now he was ready to settle for simple, short, and sweet.

All he really wanted, after all, was a date to Prom.

There was no reason it had to go down in history as the coolest ask in the history of the universe. At least, that was what Lloyd had tried to tell himself.

As Tess vanished behind him, Lloyd walked over to the row of lockers against the wall. "Hi, Kristen," he said, sounding a lot calmer than he actually felt.

She glanced up at him blankly, almost like she'd never seen him before. Things weren't off to a good start, but Lloyd pushed on anyway. "It's Lloyd," he explained, tapping himself on the chest. "I'm in your civics class."

"Really?" Kristen asked, squinting at him as she tried to remember his face.

"You lent me a pencil," Lloyd went on. "I was like, 'do you have a pencil,' and you were all, 'yeah.'" Lloyd fumbled around in his pocket and pulled out a brand-new pencil. "Well, I brought it back . . . but that's not the point, really . . ."

"Oh."

"This might seem out of the blue . . ." Lloyd continued. "It is out of the blue, actually, but Prom's coming up and I'm looking for a date and I wondered if you maybe wanted to go with me?"

"Are you serious?" Kristen asked in surprise.

"I know it's a little last minute. But I'm really fun, I

swear. I have references!" Lloyd replied.

"No, it's not that," Kristen said, shaking her head. "I have a boyfriend. Didn't you know that?"

Lloyd's face fell. "Oh. No, I guess not. Is it a new thing, or . . ."

"Sorry, this is just so weird," she said. "I thought everyone knew about us. I'm Kristen, he's Anton. We're Kranton?"

When it became clear that Lloyd still had no idea what she was talking about, Kristen flung open her locker. Enormous, glitter-covered letters spelled out KRANTON inside the door, and every single surface of the locker's interior was covered with photos of Kristen and Anton . . . as well as puffy-paint hearts in every color of the rainbow.

"How can you not know about us?" she asked. "You'd have to live in a cave. I mean, we're *always* together. This five minutes I'm talking to you is the longest we've been apart in months."

"I had no idea," Lloyd replied, mortified.

Kristen slammed her locker door closed . . . and at the same moment, she and Lloyd realized that Anton was standing on the other side of it.

"You're back!" Kristen squealed in delight.

"God, I missed you," Anton replied as he pulled her close, and they started making out like they'd been apart for five years—not five minutes.

Lloyd awkwardly tried to stick the pencil into one of Kristen's pockets but gave up pretty quickly. "Okay then," he said, stepping backward. "Talk to you around. Kranton."

As Lloyd slunk away, he realized that he was grateful for one thing: that Tess had left for her own locker on the second floor. At least there were no witnesses to his latest humiliation.

Meanwhile, Nova hurried down to the basement art room before homeroom to see if the papier-mâché she'd worked on the day before was dry. If it was still damp, she wouldn't be able to paint it for at least another day, and there simply wasn't enough time left for a delay like that.

To her surprise, the art room was completely dark. For some strange reason, the utility fluorescent lights weren't on . . . even though the rest of the school was fully illuminated. "Hello?" she called out loudly as she hovered in the doorway.

Click.

Somewhere in the darkness, a switch flipped. An ethereal glow filled the art room as the fountain's motor started to hum; water jetted through the tubes and pipes, streaming into a pool above the softly colored lights.

It was romantic.

It was beautiful.

It was unforgettable.

It was everything Nova had dreamed of for Prom.

As Nova gasped in surprise, Jesse stepped out from behind the exquisite fountain. The reflection from the water danced over his face, highlighting the question in his eyes.

"How did you—you must've worked all night," Nova marveled.

In spite of himself, Jesse grinned, and Nova smiled right back at him.

"You like it?" he asked, a trace of hesitation in his voice. Coming from someone like Nova, that meant a lot. Ever since that afternoon when she'd walked out of the art room, Jesse had started to realize that there was more to her than he'd thought. She wasn't just another Prom-obsessed airhead like so many other girls he knew.

She was special.

"Of course I like it," Nova exclaimed. "It's beautiful."

Jesse wasn't used to praise like that. He wasn't really used to praise at all.

"I have a kid brother," he said suddenly. "He's seven. And because of my mom's work schedule, I have to pick him up from school."

"Why are you telling me this?" Nova asked.

"It's why I'm late," Jesse explained. "It's why I cut class and I'm late getting here. I just want you to know I'm not blowing it off 'cause I'm a slacker."

Nova glanced at the floor. "I'm sorry I assumed that," she said quietly.

"It's okay," Jesse said as he shrugged. "Everybody does."

This time, when their eyes met across the fountain, neither one looked away.

After school, Lucas gulped down a snack on his way to the library. He wanted to find the perfect table for studying with Simone . . . out of the way, so they wouldn't have everyone staring at them during their study session, but far from the quiet section so that they could talk—quietly, of course—and hang out. By his calculations there were only about three tables in the whole library that met both qualifications, and Lucas knew that they filled up fast.

Today, though, he was in luck! Lucas strategically arranged his books across the top of the table, sat down, and looked up, practicing the perfect response for when Simone arrived. "Simone! Hey! I didn't see you there," he announced. Then Lucas made a face. "What am I saying, of course I saw her."

Across the room, a nerdy-looking guy shot him a weird look, but Lucas didn't care. Nothing could lessen his excitement about the chance to spend a few more hours alone with Simone . . . even if there was a killer chemistry test looming.

Meanwhile, Simone was on her way down the hall after a quick stop by her locker to grab her chemistry book. But before she made it to the library, Tyler eased up next to her. "Hey," he said.

"What do you want?" Simone asked without looking at him.

"Can I give you a ride home?"

"I have plans," she replied shortly.

Tyler stepped quickly to block her path. He stared into her eyes, making himself all intense and vulnerable at the same time. "I really need to talk, Simone," he said, so quietly that she had to lean a little closer to hear him. "There aren't a lot of people I can do that with. Just a few minutes."

Simone meant to step away. She meant to keep walking to the library. But somehow those dark brown eyes, filled with longing, kept her from doing the right thing. And suddenly she found herself walking alongside Tyler, in the opposite direction from the library, out to the street where his car was waiting.

And once she was in the passenger seat of Tyler's car, with her seat belt fastened, the thought of Lucas sitting alone in the library, waiting . . . and waiting . . . never even crossed her mind.

Tyler didn't drive far—just a few blocks from school, where he parked on a tree-lined street. Sunlight filtered through the bright green leaves as Simone tried to ignore the pounding of her heart. She tried to stay strong. Simone stared out the window, willing herself not to look into those gorgeous eyes again.

"Why won't you answer my texts?" Tyler got right to the point, angling in his seat to face her.

"You know why," she replied.

"Please don't ice me out like this," he said. His hand inched closer to hers. "I'm a little lost here. I know it's messed up about Jordan, but we were together a long time. She's talked about Prom for years! I'm trying not to hurt her or you. It's not easy."

"But—"

"You're such a special girl." Tyler cut her off. His voice was gentle, sincere. "If you weren't, I'd never expect you to understand."

With his eyes on her, Tyler noticed the moment her shoulders fell, and the tension around her eyes melted away. He leaned in, and this time, Simone turned toward him, searching his face, and finding exactly what she wanted to see there.

But what neither of them noticed was Jordan walking by. She watched their heads bent together, the inevitable kiss. There was plenty of time, Jordan knew, to feel hurt and betrayed and brokenhearted.

But right now, in this moment, the tears in her eyes were from anger.

As twilight started to fall, Jesse was back in the art room, stapling a strand of twinkle lights to a swirly navy backdrop. He glanced up as Nova returned, looking absolutely miserable as she ended a call. She fell into a chair near the door and buried her head in her hands. "Unbelievable," she muttered.

"What?" Jesse asked.

"Archfield's prom is this weekend, and Ali just found out their theme is Starry Starry Night," Nova said.

"They have an extra Starry. So?"

Nova shook her head. "It's going to sound really stupid," she said. "Forget it."

Jesse put down the staple gun. "Go on."

"It's like I thought we were creating this special, beautiful, one-of-a-kind night," Nova explained. "And it turns out there's another one a couple of miles away. It makes it feel . . . ordinary."

From across the room, Jesse studied her, noticing the way her shoulders slumped and her eyes looked so tired. "Well, maybe we should check out how starry their night really is," he suggested.

Nova tilted her head to the side and raised her eyebrows. She had to smile when she noticed the gleam in Jesse's eyes.

Nova knew exactly what it meant.

Jesse walked out of the art room without saying another word, and it took only a few seconds before Nova pulled herself out of the chair to follow him, all the way up the stairs, out the door, and into the parking lot. She paused when she saw his motorcycle, gleaming in the light from the setting sun.

Jesse flashed a smile at her. "Are we going the extra distance or what?" he asked.

"On this thing?" she asked, shaking her head.

"You can do it, Nova," he replied as he climbed onto the bike.

"Do what?"

Jesse tossed her a helmet; Nova caught it and clutched it tightly.

"Trust me," he said, and in those two simple words, Nova realized that she already did. She didn't know how it had happened or when, but she did. One hundred percent.

She put on the helmet, fastened it beneath her chin, and climbed onto the bike behind Jesse. At first, her hands around his waist were tentative and unsure, but as Jesse revved the engine and the bike zoomed off, she held on with all her strength. It was such a rush—the blur of the streetlights and the sting of the wind and the smell of his aftershave. She tried to hide her exhilaration but didn't really care that she failed.

That was another first for Nova.

It was dark when they reached Archfield, and the

school had the lonely, empty air of a Friday night, when everybody had cleared out for the weekend. Dodging the puddles of light along the walkways, Nova and Jesse crept up to a side door. She stopped and stared at the heavy chain and padlock securing it. Was their adventure about to end already?

"How are you gonna get us in there?" whispered Nova.

Jesse's eyes narrowed as he examined the door, the lock, the brick wall. "I'm gonna fire my grappling-hook gun, scale the side of this wall, and crash in through the skylights," he finally said.

"Really?" Nova gasped.

Jesse shot her a look. "No."

She followed his gaze to another door, just twenty feet away, which was propped open by a janitor's bucket and mop.

"Oh. Good thinking," Nova said.

They slipped through the door and silently made their way through the halls of Archfield High until they stumbled upon the gym. After glancing in every direction to make sure they truly were alone, Jesse held a finger to his lips . . . and pushed open the door.

For a moment, neither of them spoke. Jesse's

footsteps echoed through the gym as he evaluated the decorations.

"Oh, man," he finally said. "This is pathetic."

Nova started to smile as Jesse flicked at a cheap cardboard star hanging from the ceiling. "These totally come in a kit," he said. "Lame. And a balloon column, really?"

Nova's smiled turned into a smirk as Jesse grew more and more critical.

"Those twinkle lights don't twinkle," he continued. "And where's their cosmic canopy?"

"Amateurs," Nova said, mimicking his mocking tone. He turned to her, smiling sheepishly.

"Why are you doing this?" asked Nova.

Jesse shrugged, trying to slip back into his usual attitude. "Eh. I hadn't broken in anywhere for a while, so—"

"I'm serious," she interrupted him. "You don't care about this. Why help me?"

"It's nice to be around someone who believes in something so much," Jesse replied.

Neither of them had expected that level of honesty. Nova, a little unnerved, took a step backwards—and

bumped into a rickety column of sparkly stars. It toppled over with a loud crash!

Nova and Jesse started to crack up as they scrambled to fix the column, and suddenly—when she looked
back on this moment, Nova couldn't quite figure out
how it happened—they were almost in each other's
arms, standing so close that Nova could smell his hair
and see the way his eyelashes cast fragile shadows on his
cheeks. It was the kind of moment, she realized as her
heart started to race, when a kiss could happen.

Not could—*should*.

She drew back sharply. "What are you doing?"

"What do you mean?"

"You were gonna kiss me!"

"No, I wasn't!"

Nova blinked. "Why not?"

"*What?*" Jesse asked in disbelief. "Nova, if I'm about
to kiss you, you'll know it."

She wanted to argue—she was ready to argue—but
a sudden commotion from the hallway stopped them
both. At the far end of the gym, a door creaked open.

"Somebody there?" the janitor called out, his keys
jangling.

Nova and Jesse looked at each other with wide eyes. "We gotta go!" he whispered as he grabbed her hand. They ducked out of the gym just as the janitor's flashlight beamed over the polished wood floors and sparkly stars.

But they were in such a rush that they didn't think to cushion the closing door. It shut with a slam that reverberated through the gym, and in that instant the janitor started running after them.

Out of breath, exhilarated, somehow terrified and thrilled at the same time, Nova and Jesse raced through the school, down hallways, through the cafeteria kitchen, and over the empty stage in the auditorium, stopping only once when Nova noticed one of the few prom posters on the wall.

"Black and white?" she asked in disbelief.

"Come on!" Jesse said as he grabbed her hand again and pulled her away. They ended up close to where they'd started, cornered in a locker room attached to the gym, pressed against the cold tile wall of the showers. The janitor's footsteps were approaching. Nova and Jesse were about to get busted—big time.

Then Jesse pointed over their heads to a narrow rectangular window.

Nova took one look at the window and shook her head: no way. There was *no way* she was going to climb through that tiny window near the ceiling.

Jesse nodded in response. He knew it was their only option—and so did Nova when the beam from the janitor's flashlight shone over the tile. In an instant, she scrambled onto Jesse's shoulders, and with the help of a sharp push from him she propelled herself through the window. Jesse hoisted himself up to follow her. When he landed on the ground, they both took off running again, not stopping until they reached Jesse's bike. The rev of the engine drowned out the janitor's shouting as he lumbered out of the school, still trying to catch them.

As the bike tore down the street, Nova yelled in triumph, "We are so hard-core!"

But at that moment, the darkness around lit up with flashing red lights. Jesse recognized them before Nova did. He steered the motorcycle over to the side of the road as a police car pulled up behind them.

So hard-core?

More like so busted!

CHAPTER

ELEVEN

Sitting on the curb, Nova shielded her eyes from the glare of the police car's high beams. She couldn't understand how Jesse was able to sit there so calmly while the officer filled out paperwork in his cruiser.

"I've got a record now," Nova groaned. "A rap sheet. I have *priors*."

"You don't have priors," Jesse pointed out. "A stern warning and a call to your parents isn't exactly your first strike."

But Nova wasn't listening. "What if they tell Georgetown?" she said, worried.

"Nova. It's fine," he said patiently. "It's just—"

The flash of headlights and the squeal of brakes cut him off as Frank's pick-up truck wheeled to a stop. The door flew up as Frank burst out of the truck. "You!" he bellowed, pointing at Jesse. "What did you do to her?"

Nova leaped to her feet. "Dad. Dad. It's okay," she said.

"Okay?" Frank repeated. "Are you out of your mind?"

"Dad. He was doing all this for me," Nova tried to explain.

"Breaking into a school!" raged Frank. "Getting stopped by the cops!"

"Dad, please listen. I deserve the blame," Nova insisted.

"Really? Whose idea was it?" Frank asked.

"You're right," Jesse said to Frank. "It was my idea."

Frank glared at Jesse and then turned to his daughter. "This isn't you, Nova," Frank said firmly as he grabbed her hand. "Let's go."

On Monday morning at school, Corey and Lucas were shuffling books into their lockers when Simone unexpectedly approached them. Lucas knew, of course, the moment she approached. His senses were always on high alert whenever Simone was near.

"Hi," she said, sounding a little nervous.

"Oh, hey, Simone," Lucas said, the fake casualness in his voice obvious to everyone. "Didn't see you there."

Simone got right to the point. "I'm really sorry I didn't make it to the library to study with you," she said, apologizing.

Behind her, Corey's eyes almost bugged out of his head. This was big news. Why hadn't Lucas bothered to tell him that Simone had stood him up?

Lucas's face froze into a mask of surprise. "We were supposed to study?" he said. "Wow. You know, I totally forgot."

"Really?" Simone asked. She was pretty sure this was a lie, but some small part of her hoped it was true—because then she wouldn't have to keep feeling so guilty for deserting him on Friday.

"Yeah," Lucas said, shaking his head and trying to laugh. "That's crazy. I was out with the team that night. Tyler wanted to show me some moves. Varsity stuff. I'm looking good for next year, so . . ."

"Tyler showed you," Simone said slowly.

"Yeah. We must've lost track of time. I forgot all about our plans," Lucas said.

"Well, I'm still sorry," Simone replied. "I would've

hated to be waiting all afternoon for someone to show up."

"Yeah," Lucas said, turning back to his locker. "That would've sucked." She now felt about a thousand times worse.

Standing off to the side, overhearing every word, Corey could do nothing but feel his buddy's pain. Whatever had gone wrong—whatever had gotten in the way—it was between Lucas and Simone.

And he was *not* going to get involved.

By the end of the school day, Lucas hadn't cheered up at all, and Corey was starting to get worried. None of his usual jokes or witty commentary had pulled Lucas out of his funk, so Corey decided to let Lucas know just how deeply he understood his hurt.

"This is awful," Corey announced on the way to their lockers. "You've been dissed, trampled, humiliated, stomped on—"

"I get it," Lucas said shortly. "Okay?"

Both boys stopped as they noticed an envelope taped to Lucas's locker door.

"What is that?" Corey asked, peering over Lucas's shoulder.

Lucas glanced around and saw Simone standing across the hallway, a suspicious smile on her lips. "Hey, Simone," he said, hoping she hadn't heard Corey's rant. "You didn't happen to see anybody tape this envelope onto my locker, did you?"

"Why, what is it?" Simone asked innocently. But her smile wasn't fooling anyone.

Lucas ripped open the envelope and peeked inside. "Tickets," he realized. "To see Closet Monster?"

Corey sniffed loudly. "They had an interesting single, but then they changed bass players on their second album and ended up sucking. This is kind of random."

"Yeah, their second album was pretty lame," Simone said casually. "I don't even know why Stick Hippo's opening for them."

"What?!" Lucas and Corey gasped at the same time. They looked at each other in disbelief, then turned to Simone.

"How did you know about this?" Corey demanded. "I'm a certified Stick Hippo webmaster and I don't even know about it!"

"It's kind of a secret gig." She shrugged. "I like your site, by the way."

"You're the one hit," Corey realized.

"She's the one hit!" Lucas echoed gleefully.

"Wait," Corey said. "That means my mom is lying."

"I bet they're great live," Simone said to Lucas with one of those smiles that made his stomach do somersaults.

"Are you kidding? They're the best!" Corey exclaimed. "Where are our seats?"

Lucas pulled the tickets out of the envelope.

There were only two.

Corey knew what that meant. Even if he didn't, the uncomfortable look on Simone's face would have told him. "This is like a 'you guys' thing, huh?" he said. "That's cool. Just, uh, get me a T-shirt, or something."

He slammed his locker closed and tried to act like he didn't care, but he shouldn't have wasted his time. At that moment, Lucas could only think of Simone.

Sitting cross-legged on the floor, Mei leaned against her locker door, feeling the cold metal through her T-shirt. She flipped through the packet of papers in her lap, concentrating so deeply that she didn't even notice that Justin had arrived.

"Hey!" he said as he plunked down on the floor next to her.

Mei jumped in surprise, then quickly flipped the packet over so Justin couldn't see it.

"You okay?" he asked as he slid closer to her.

"Yeah. Totally," Mei said, sounding flustered. She gestured to the packet. "AP English."

"Uch," Justin replied, making a face. "This might cheer you up."

There was something shiny in his hand. Mei reached for it and held it in front of her face. Dozens of tiny charms dangled from a delicate bracelet; they caught the light and reflected it back at her.

"It's my mom's," Justin explained. "My dad gave it to her for their prom. Anyway, I'd be really proud if you would wear it."

"Oh, Justin," Mei breathed. "It's beautiful."

"I did make one little addition," Justin said, grinning as he pointed to a charm in the shape of a tiny letter M. "For Michigan. Next year."

The smile vanished from Mei's face. Suddenly the beautiful bracelet was transformed into something much bigger; the charms on it carried the weight of promises she wasn't sure she could keep. Mei thrust the bracelet back at him. "Wait, didn't you say you were getting me a wrist corsage?" she asked. "Wouldn't that be, like, weird? To wear both? Plus I don't know if it'll match my earrings, and it might jangle when we dance. Or fall off."

Justin struggled not to show his emotions. "Oh," he said, trying to sound calm and cool. "I guess I didn't think of that."

He shoved the bracelet in his pocket and looked away. But Mei had known him for too long to miss how angry—and hurt—he was.

And that made her even more miserable.

Tyler strolled down the hall toward Jordan's locker. He'd just realized that he hadn't really seen her all day, which was kind of weird. As usual, it was easy to find her, surrounded by a ton of friends. But the moment they saw Tyler approaching, all the girls scattered, leaving only Jordan. Her back was to him.

"Hey, babe," Tyler called out.

When she turned around, her face was like stone. Tyler had seen that look before. "Uh-oh," he said, trying to make light of it. "What'd I do now?"

"It's over, Tyler," she replied. "I know about your sophomore."

"I gave her a ride home," Tyler said smoothly. "What are you upset about?"

"I'm not upset," Jordan said, and as the words left her mouth she realized they were true. "I'm done."

Tyler started to realize just how serious the situation was. "You don't mean that. Prom's right around the corner," he said. "What happened to 'Prom is our moment?' What are you gonna do? Not go?"

Jordan faltered, momentarily distracted by doubt. She'd spent the entire weekend imagining this scene, but somehow the reality of Prom without Tyler had never occurred to her.

But it was too late to turn back now.

"Don't worry about me, Tyler," Jordan said. "You just keep worrying about you, since that's all you're good at, anyway."

She spun around and walked away, her heart shuddering in her chest, her eyes full of worry. But she knew, as she walked, that she had made the right decision—and done the right thing.

Tyler stood, suddenly alone, watching her leave. A plan started to form in his mind.

It was the only way he could think of to save the situation . . . for himself, at least.

CHAPTER

★ ☆ TWELVE ☆ ★

When Jesse pulled up at his brother's elementary school, he noticed right away that something was different. Today, Charlie wasn't playing with his usual buddies. Instead, he was proudly showing off his collection of vintage baseball cards to a tall, gorgeous teenage girl.

Nova.

They were so engrossed in the cards that neither one noticed Jesse as he approached.

"This Harvey Kuenn rookie card's worth, like, forty bucks, and this Al Kaline would go for eighty at least!" Charlie told Nova excitedly.

She whistled. "You must have some allowance, kid!" Nova teased him.

"My dad left them behind," Charlie said matter-of-factly.

Nova nodded slowly as another piece of the Jesse puzzle was revealed to her.

"Charlie," Jesse called out, not looking at Nova. "Why are you carrying those around? They stay in the basement."

He grabbed the cards away from Charlie; the harshness in his voice made Charlie stare at the ground. Then Jesse turned to Nova. "What are you doing here?"

"I came to apologize," she replied. "I was wrong. And I'm sorry."

"You came all the way here to tell me that?" Jesse asked.

"Yeah," Nova said. "I even ditched last period."

Charlie glanced up at Jesse.

"For her, that's a big deal," Jesse told his little brother.

"I thought I knew you, Jesse. I don't," she continued. "But I'd like to. If you'd let me."

There was silence as they looked at each other. Suddenly, Charlie spoke up. "Hold on," he said to Nova. "What are you? His peer-counselor or something?"

Jesse grabbed Charlie and started to ruffle his hair, making the little boy dissolve into giggles. Over Charlie's head, Jesse and Nova exchanged a smile.

Driving her car behind Jesse's motorcycle, Nova followed the brothers over to the diner where their mom worked. They sat at the long counter as Sandra served them tall, frosty milk shakes topped with whipped cream.

Nova eyed Jesse's milk shake. "Coffee. With a cherry?" she asked. "Interesting."

"Shut up," he replied playfully.

"You say you two have been working together at school?" Sandra asked as she leaned against the counter.

"Something like that," Jesse said mysteriously as he and Nova exchanged another grin. It was like now that they had cleared the air, everything seemed better. Smoother. Happier.

At that moment, the room filled with laughter from a booth against the opposite wall. Everyone turned to see a group of college students building a food tower—sandwiches stacked on pizza, topped with chocolate cake, condiments oozing over the whole mess. Suddenly it toppled over, spilling food everywhere. The guys cracked up.

"My favorite kind of customers," Sandra sighed as she reached for a rag.

"Oh, waitress!" called one of the boys.

"Clean-up on aisle five!" cracked another.

Jesse twisted around to face the table as his muscles tensed up. "You gonna clean that up?" he asked sharply.

The college students ignored him.

Nova reached for Jesse's arm. "Why don't we get out of here?" she asked in a low voice.

"That's a good idea, Nova," Sandra said at once. "I'll keep Charlie here; you two should go."

But Jesse was already on his way over to the college kids' table.

"Are you going to clean that up?" he asked, louder this time.

"Do you guys hear something?" one of the college guys asked, grinning at his friend.

"I don't hear anything," his friend replied. "I don't see anything, either."

The guys cracked up, high-fiving over the huge mess they'd made.

Jesse clenched his fists as he stepped toward them, but Nova ducked in front of him just in time. Their eyes locked.

"I want you to come with me," she said with quiet intensity.

Jesse glanced at the guys, then looked back into her eyes.

"You can do this, Jesse, I know you can," she continued.

"Do what?" he asked.

"Trust me," she replied.

Nova could sense his hesitation. So she reached out, grabbed his hand, and led him from the restaurant.

Sandra breathed a sigh of relief, grateful that Nova had been able to defuse the situation. She strolled over to the messy table as the college kids got up to leave.

"Boys not happy with your meal?" she asked lightly.

"It was great," one of the guys replied with a smirk. "Little messy, though."

"Hey, Charlie," Sandra called over her shoulder as she began the epic cleanup. "What is it they say about people who play with their food?"

Charlie took a long sip of his milk shake as he spun around on the stool. "They generally have a low I.Q." he piped up. "Can you top me off, Barb?"

As the other customers started to laugh at the obnoxious college students, Sandra winked at Charlie.

Whenever things got rocky, she could always count on her sons—both of them.

Out in the parking lot, Nova could tell how badly Jesse wanted to storm back into the diner and teach those guys a lesson. "Those idiots *aren't* worth it," she said firmly. "Come on. They'll get what's coming to them eventually. Stuff balances out."

"Wake up, Nova," Jesse replied.

"What does that mean?"

"It's easy to believe in that stuff when everything always goes your way," he said.

A sudden flash of anger replaced the happiness she'd been feeling just moments before. "You think everything goes my way?" she snapped. "That it all just comes easy? That I have no problems in my life because my dad didn't leave?"

Jesse's face went a shade paler, but that didn't stop Nova. "Everyone has problems, Jesse," she continued. "You think sometimes I don't wanna forget everything, get on my motorcycle all angry and misunderstood and go beat some people up? I have to work my butt off just to *try* to get things to go my way. Everybody does."

Nova took a deep breath as she waited for Jesse to respond. Suddenly, to her surprise, he laughed.

"What?" she asked.

"I bet you could beat some people up," Jesse replied.

"Yeah, I could!" Nova exclaimed. She started to laugh with him. "Now, let's go dress shopping!"

"Wait . . . what?" Jesse asked, confused.

But Nova was already unlocking her car; all he could do was follow her. As Jesse climbed into the passenger seat, he looked around. The inside of Nova's car was like a secret window into her life. School papers on the floor, an old hoodie jammed between the seats, the backseat piled high with stacks of books. And something Jesse hadn't seen in a car before: dozens of "Hello, My Name Is Nova Prescott" sticker name tags. They were stuck all over the dashboard and glove compartment. There was even one in the center of the steering wheel. Some of them were yellow-edged and tattered; some were losing their stick and starting to curl up at the edges. But what was really amazing was the sheer number of them.

"You collect these things?" Jesse asked, gesturing at the name tags.

"Kind of," Nova replied as she pulled out of the parking lot. "Whenever I go to an event—a college tour, scholarship dinner, awards banquet—I always just stick 'em here afterwards. Helps remind me who I am, what I'm working toward. I guess it's kinda goofy."

"No," Jesse said, shaking his head. "No. It's really impressive."

"Yeah, well, it's been a busy year," she said, staring ahead at the road.

Jesse just nodded, totally overwhelmed by her.

In a few minutes, Nova pulled into the parking lot of her favorite boutique. It was safe to say that Jesse had never been there before. Surrounded by mirrors, pink, and sparkles, he looked completely uncomfortable—and completely out of place. Luckily, a kind employee directed him over to a large armchair just outside the dressing room and offered him a cup of tea. Jesse turned down the tea, but he gladly settled into the chair for what he suspected would be a long afternoon.

Soon Nova disappeared into the dressing room, her arms filled with all sorts of dresses. One at a time, she tried them on and modeled them for Jesse. A pink frilly dress that made her look a little like a cupcake got a big thumbs-down from him. The next one, a polka-dot nightmare, was so bad it made Jesse shield his eyes. When she emerged from the dressing room in a flow-ery monstrosity of a muumuu, Jesse laughed out loud.

Nova took one look at herself in the three-way mirror and ran for cover.

Jesse decided it was time to help Nova out. He grabbed a superslinky black dress that wasn't much more than a scrap of fabric and passed it to her around the dressing-room curtain. She shoved it back at him immediately. His version of "helping" was *not* helpful.

Jesse leaned against the wall as Nova tried on another dress behind the curtain. "So how come you don't have a date?" he asked.

"He bailed on me," she replied.

"Well, there must be somebody else you could go with," Jesse said. "Like, the class president or something?"

Nova stuck her head around the curtain. "I'm the class president."

"How 'bout the VP? Treasurer?" Jesse suggested. "Come on. There must be an honor student out there who—"

Jesse stopped talking as Nova emerged from the dressing room. She was in a gorgeous peach and gold, strapless, lace dress that seemed made especially for her. His heart pounded oddly, and he suddenly felt wildly out of place.

"Um . . ." he stammered.

"Really?" she asked, hardly believing that the dress was *that* perfect. Or did the "um" translate as "you look like a cow"?

Apparently, perfect was the statement.

The salesgirl swooped in, eager to seal the deal. "That looks fantastic with our amethyst pendant necklace!"

"Necklace? Please," laughed Nova, looking at the tag. "With the price of this dress, the only necklace I can afford will be made of candy." She stared at her reflection in the mirror, oblivious to the way Jesse was looking at her.

"That guy who ditched you made a big mistake," he said as soon as he was capable of stringing words together again.

Nova turned around to smile at him and was suddenly very aware of his eyes on her. Jesse's expression told her that this was, without a doubt, *the* Prom dress for her.

And there was something else in his eyes, something that Nova had detected over the last few days, small flickers that made her wonder, just a little, before she pushed the thoughts far from her mind.

But right now, in front of the full-length mirror, there was no room for wondering. Jesse's feelings were written all over his face.

At the same time, Mei was trying on her Prom dress, too, in the little bathroom attached to her bedroom. She stared at her reflection in the mirror, absolutely miserable. Everything was such a wreck—her dress, her hair, her life. These problems were too big for her to fix.

Justin knocked softly on the door—again. "Can I at least just see it on you?" he asked.

"No!" Mei called back. "I look like a manatee! No one will ever see this dress on me!" She ripped off the gown and got dressed in her regular clothes again. Then she burst out of the bathroom, the prom dress crumpled into a ball between her hands. "The color is wrong, the cut is wrong, the fabric is wrong. Everything is wrong!"

She shoved the dress into a too-small trash can in the corner of her bedroom; it spilled over the sides pathetically. She punched at the fancy material, trying to cram it back into the trash.

"No . . . don't . . . Mei . . ." Justin said helplessly. "Now what are you gonna wear?"

"I don't know!" she snapped angrily. "Nothing!"

Justin's face filled with concern. He took a deep breath while he waited for Mei to calm down a little. Then he finally asked, "What is this about? I know you. It's not about a dress."

As he waited for her to say something, Justin could tell how much she was struggling. He and Mei were so close that suddenly Justin was sure he knew what was coming. He swallowed hard, fighting back the feeling of dread.

If it had to happen, he just wanted to get it over with already.

"Look," he said, his voice a little shaky. "If you don't want to go, you can just tell me. We can skip this whole Promzilla routine."

"What are you talking about?"

"First it was Mark and Isabella, then the bracelet, now the dress," Justin rattled off examples of Mei's recent weirdness. "You're obviously looking for excuses not to go."

"I never said that," she argued.

"You don't have to," he replied. "I know when I'm being blown off. You don't want to go, fine. Prom's off, problem solved."

Justin didn't wait to hear Mei's response. He didn't think he could keep it together for another minute. He stormed out of Mei's bedroom, leaving Mei standing there, alone, wondering how she'd made such a mess of everything that mattered to her.

CHAPTER

★ ♥ ★THIRTEEN ★ ♥ ★

That evening, Simone was helping her mom make dinner when the doorbell rang. She dried her hands on a dish towel and hurried into the hallway. But by the time Simone got to the door, no one was there. Frowning, she glanced down . . . and noticed something strange: there were two rocks on the doorstep. One was enormous, with the word NO painted on it. Next to it, a tiny pebble read YES.

There was an envelope between the two rocks.

Simone reached for the envelope in confusion and opened it. There was a note inside that said:

Prom? Bring me your answer.

There was something else on the note, too—a big, bold arrow pointing toward the front yard. Simone glanced up to see Tyler step out from behind a tree. He started walking toward her.

"What are you doing?" Simone asked as her heart started to beat a little faster.

"Can't a guy ask a girl to Prom?" Tyler asked with a shrug.

"I thought you were going with Jordan."

"It's over," he said. "For real. I ended it."

"Tyler . . ." she began, unsure.

"You can just bring your answer to school tomorrow if you wanna think about it," Tyler replied as he gestured at the rocks.

Simone smiled. The huge rock was way too heavy for her to carry anywhere.

"Oh, and I got you this, too," Tyler added. He reached into his back pocket and pulled out a small jewelry box. Simone opened it to find a guitar pick nestled inside. "I'd love to hear you play sometime."

Simone's smile widened.

How could she say no to that?

After somehow keeping it together through a long afternoon of cheerleading practice and the smothering attention of her friends, Jordan finally got home. She knew that they meant well, but all Jordan really wanted was to be alone. Her plans that night were simple: climb into bed and sleep for as long possible. The day had been exhausting in every way.

But before she crawled under the covers, Jordan noticed something: her full-length mirror, practically covered in photos of Tyler and her from happier days. One by one she had added those photos over the months, chronicling all the romantic dates and awesome parties they had attended . . . as a couple. Looking at that mirror, Jordan suddenly understood—*really* understood—that there would be no more photos. Because there was no more Jordan and Tyler.

And keeping the pictures up would be as fake as their relationship had turned out to be.

"Good-bye, Tyler," Jordan said softly as she reached for one of the pictures. She pulled it off the mirror and dropped it in the trash. Then she pulled off another, and another, and another, getting a whole new burst of energy and enthusiasm as more of the mirror was revealed.

Jordan soon reached the last photo. Her hand hovered over it for a moment; Jordan knew that when she pulled it off, the mirror would be empty, a blank panel in her room.

But Jordan was wrong about that. The photo-free mirror wasn't empty at all. Her own face was staring back at her.

"Hey, Jordan," her younger sister, Janel, said as she passed by the room. "Are you—whoa!" Janel's voice broke off as she stared at the photo-free mirror. For a moment, the sisters stood together without talking. Then Janel said, "I like it better that way."

"Me, too," Jordan replied. She smiled into the mirror and knew, all of a sudden, that everything was going to be okay.

During free period the next day, Lloyd went to the library to get some studying done. He spent ne whole period at an empty table in the cor he remembered that he had to check o

English class. As he ambled down the aisle looking for it, a girl nearby dropped a book on the table. "Do *all* assigned books have to be so torturously boring?" she asked, sighing in frustration.

Lloyd looked around, but didn't see anyone—beside himself—who she could have been talking to. He glanced at the book and made a face of solidarity when he recognized the cover. "Ugh, this is rough. *Ethan Frome*?"

"The worst!" the girl exclaimed. "Guy falls in love with his wife's cousin, goes sledding with her, she winds up paralyzed. Snore."

"That's an incredibly accurate plot summary," Lloyd said, and they both started to laugh. A spark of connection passed between them, and in that moment Lloyd decided to go for it—just as the bell rang. The girl started to gather up her books, and Lloyd knew that he had to act fast.

"Listen, you don't happen to have a date to Prom, do you?" he asked.

"Me?" she said shyly.

"Yeah," Lloyd replied. "I mean, I know it's a crazy—"

"No, it's really sweet," the girl interrupted him. "I don't think we've ever talked before . . . have we?"

"Maybe not," Lloyd said, smiling. "I'm Lloyd."

"Betsy," the girl said.

"Short for Elizabeth?"

"That's right."

"Pretty," Lloyd said, and Betsy's smile lit up her whole face.

"Thanks."

"So what do you say, Bets?" he said, his confidence growing. "Prom?"

"That could be fun," Betsy replied. "You seem nice."

A huge grin spread across Lloyd's face. Then he realized that Betsy wasn't finished talking.

"But I have a date already," she continued. "I mean it's just a friend; we're going as friends . . . but Prom's Saturday. I can't cancel now."

"No, I understand," Lloyd replied, trying to keep smiling without looking like a lunatic . . . or like someone who'd just had his hopes crushed beneath a steamroller.

"It's too bad," Betsy added regretfully. "Maybe if we'd met sooner, you know?"

Lloyd nodded, overwhelmed by the knowledge that once again, he was just a little too late.

Luckily, Betsy didn't seem to notice how hard he

was taking it. "Isn't that funny, how you can go to school with somebody for so long and not even meet them 'til now?"

"Yeah. Funny," Lloyd said, trying to come up with a joke. "Like sledding and being paralyzed."

If Betsy had known him for longer than five minutes, she would have heard the strain in his voice.

And recognized the disappointment in his eyes.

After school that day, Ali was on her way to Nova's house when she spotted a familiar face in the tuxedo shop on Emerson Street. Even better, he was examining the material of a gaudy tuxedo jacket. Ali started to grin as she walked into the store.

"Tactile," Rolo said as he pulled on the hideous jacket.

"Rolo. Wow," Ali said. "That's a good look for you. You thinking rental? Or will you and 'Athena' be attending a series of formal events?"

Rolo stared at himself in the mirror. He looked a little lost. "How do I know which one to pick?"

"Hmm," Ali replied, humoring him. "Well, do you know what Athena's wearing?"

"Oh. This," Rolo said as he pulled a piece of paper

out of his pocket. Ali unfolded it to reveal a page torn out of a magazine. It had a picture of a gorgeous super-model wearing a dress that was a little too short, a little too tight, and a little too grown-up for any of the girls at Brookside to pull off.

"Nice try," Ali laughed.

"What do you mean?" asked Rolo.

"First of all, this dress is fit and flare," Ali pointed out. "You'd have to be a Victoria's Secret model to pull this off."

"That's what she's wearing," Rolo insisted.

"Right," she said sarcastically. "I'll give you points for taste. If I was someone's imaginary girlfriend, I would totally wear this. What magazine did you rip this out of?"

"She sent it to me."

"In the mail. Of course," said Ali. "Because her e-mail privileges were revoked when she stayed out . . . clubbing."

"Clubbing," Rolo said at the same time. "Exactly."

Ali gave up. "All right, Rolo," she said, sighing in frustration. "I guess I'll see you guys at Prom."

"Cool," Rolo said, smiling obliviously.

Ali shook her head as she pushed open the door

to leave. On her way out, she passed by Tyler, Derek, and Max. The guys didn't take long to pick out a few tux styles to try on. But they stopped short when they got to entrance of the dressing rooms—and found Jesse struggling with the cuffs of a tuxedo shirt.

"Richter?" Tyler asked in surprise. "Man, what are you doing here?"

"Dude, are you going to Prom?" Derek said.

"No way Richter's going to Prom," Max replied.

Jesse ignored them as he buttoned the shirt.

"Maybe he's got a job as, like, an usher or something!" Derek said with a smirk.

Jesse shot Derek a look—until he remembered what Nova had said at the diner the other day. He'd realized that she was right: those guys weren't worth it.

And these guys weren't, either.

"Shut up, Derek," Tyler said. Then he turned to Jesse. "Dude, seriously, who's the lucky girl?"

"Maybe it's Nova Prescott," Max cracked. "They fell in love making centerpieces!"

All the guys burst out laughing. Then Tyler caught a glimpse of Jesse's face in the mirror. "Wait . . . no way . . . it *is* Nova!" he realized.

"Nova and Jesse?" exclaimed Max. "That's hilarious!"

"What are you gonna do when she goes to college?" Derek sneered. "Sleep on her floor?"

"Would you *shut up*?" Tyler said again. He turned back to Jesse. "Really, man, you and Nova, good luck with that. . . ."

But a smile was already playing at the corners of his mouth . . . the kind of smile that was seconds away from turning into a laugh. And once Tyler started to laugh, his friends joined in. They were still cracking up as they disappeared into their dressing rooms.

"That fits nicely," a saleslady said as she approached Jesse. "Are you ready to try a jacket?"

"Um, not right now," Jesse replied. Barely controlling his anger, he fought to undo the stupid buttons on the shirt.

Jesse couldn't get it off fast enough.

When Ali arrived at Nova's house, Mei was already there. "Finally!" Mei exclaimed as she grinned at Ali across the room. "She wouldn't even let me see it until you got here."

"Well, I should hope not," Ali replied. She whipped

out her cell phone and got ready to take a picture. "Okay, Nova, go get changed. I'm all ready to document the big reveal."

"No, no." Nova laughed. "No pictures. I'm not trying it on—I'll just hold it up on the hanger." She opened her closet door and carefully pulled out the gorgeous prom dress she'd tried on for Jesse earlier that week.

A little shyly, Nova held the dress in front of her. "Well?" she asked, turning around to show Mei and Ali. "What do you think?"

"Ooooh," Mei and Ali squealed together.

"You're going to look *amazing*," added Mei. "That dress is so perfect for you."

"Thank you!" Nova grinned. She looked in the mirror, her gaze coming to rest on her shoes. "I wonder if they'll be too high. I don't want to be taller than him."

Ali's eyebrows shot up. "Taller than who? Who? Who?" she demanded.

Nova's eyes were sparkling when she turned around to face her friends. The look on her face was unmistakable.

"You got a Prom date and this is the first we're hearing about it?" Mei shrieked.

"He hasn't asked me yet," Nova replied. "But

tomorrow's our last day working together. And I think he's going to."

"Is she talking about Jesse Richter?" Mei asked Ali before turning to Nova. "Are you talking about Jesse Richter?"

All three girls screamed at the same time—so loud and so long that dogs all over the neighborhood started barking!

"Wow!" Mei gushed. "Nova likes bad boys. Who knew?"

"You rebel," Ali teased Nova.

But Nova shook her head. "It's more than that," she replied. "It's real. I mean, I've never felt like this . . ." With a giddy squeal of glee, Nova dropped her dress and jumped onto the bed next to Ali and Mei. They bounced around, shrieking and laughing about Nova's hot new crush.

In the hallway, Nova's dad smiled as he approached her bedroom door. Frank was about to knock when he thought better of interrupting the three friends. But he couldn't help overhearing what Mei said when they all settled down.

"Wow," she repeated, still marveling at the big news. "You and Jesse Richter. I don't believe it."

"No one will," said Ali.

"Why not?" Nova asked defensively.

"Um, because you're you," Mei pointed out. "And he's . . ."

"Not exactly . . . Brandon," Ali finished for her.

"He's kinda on the other side of the planet from Brandon," Mei added.

"Well, maybe that stuff isn't as important as I thought it was," Nova said, growing serious. "Maybe there's more to a person than being valedictorian . . . or class president."

In the hallway, Frank closed his eyes as a wave of worry overcame him. His smile disappeared as he faced one of his worst fears. Then, on silent footsteps, he set off down the hall, checking to make sure he had his car keys and his wallet.

The very first time Frank had held Nova, on that beautiful day when she'd been born, he had sworn that he would always do whatever it took to protect her.

And even though eighteen years had passed and that sweet little baby girl was almost grown up, he wasn't about to break that promise.

Even if it broke Nova's heart.

CHAPTER

✦ ❥ ✧ FOURTEEN ✦ ♥ ✦

Just before his evening shift at the grocery store began, Jesse trolled the candy aisle, looking for the one kind of candy he'd never bought in his life. He grinned when he found it, thinking about who he would give it to . . . and how. Then he ambled over to the checkout aisle, where he paid for the candy with a crumpled dollar bill.

"No bag," he said to the cashier as he slipped the thin cellophane package into his pocket. Then Jesse cut through the store to the loading dock in the back, knowing that all those crates of food and produce wouldn't unload themselves. When Jesse reached for the first box, he put his hand over his pocket and felt the candy necklace inside it. Just knowing it was there made him smile.

Then he heard someone call his name.

It was Frank.

"Hello, Jesse," he said as he approached the platform.

"Hey," Jesse replied, a note of suspicion already in his voice.

"I'm here about Nova," Frank continued.

"She all right?" Jesse asked at once, a wave of worry rushing over him.

"She's fine," Frank replied. "In fact, she's better than fine. She's at the top of her class, full scholarship for next year. Big plans."

Jesse put the box down, the worry ebbing to be replaced by the first stirrings of anger. "I know."

"Okay. You know," Frank said. "But maybe you don't know how much work she's done to get to where she is. And she's in the home stretch now. That's where you came in. Right at the end."

Jesse's eyes looked weary. He knew what was coming next. "You don't even know me," he said.

"I do know you," Frank said, nodding. "I was just like you. Struggling to get by, angry at the world, no plan for the future. You might even figure it out, but it's not fair to drag Nova down while you do."

From the way Jesse refused to meet his eyes, Frank knew his words were hitting him hard. He pressed on, just to make sure that Jesse got the message.

"I know you think you can be part of her world right now," Frank continued. "Guys like us always do. But believe me when I tell you the best thing we can do for her is just stay out of her way."

Frank waited for Jesse to reply, but Jesse said nothing. In his heart, he couldn't deny that he secretly agreed with Nova's dad.

"If you care about her as much as I think you do, you won't be the thing that holds her back," Frank finished.

Then he turned and walked away.

Jesse forced himself to pick up the box again. He felt the candy necklace shift in his pocket, but it didn't bring a smile to his face anymore. Buying it was a waste, just like thinking that he and Nova could actually have something together. Something special.

It was all just a waste.

After last period the next day, Corey was talking non-stop to Lucas as they walked out of class. "So I said 'why isn't there an app that's like Fantasy Band Rotisserie?' And he goes, 'who would care?' And I was like, 'are you serious?'"

Lucas stared down the hall, looking for someone, only half listening to Corey. Then he spotted her. "Oh! There's Simone!" he exclaimed. "I gotta talk to her. Catch you later!"

Lucas practically sprinted away, leaving Corey in the middle of his story.

"Hey!" Lucas said excitedly as he fell into step with Simone.

"Hey, Lucas . . ." she replied. He had no idea what was coming, and it killed her to do it to him . . . but not enough to change her mind. She braced herself for an awful conversation.

"So on Saturday, what do you think? Pick you up at six?" he asked.

"Actually, I've been looking for you . . ." Simone began. She sighed heavily. "I need to talk to you about that. Because, well, Saturday's Prom."

Lucas's smile started to waver. Maybe he *did* know what was coming. Maybe he could sense it in the stiffness of her shoulders, in the way her eyes seemed so unsure.

"And . . . remember that guy I told you about? Who wasn't available?"

"Yeah . . ."

"Well, now he is," Simone finished lamely. "And he asked, and we're . . . going."

"Oh."

In that moment, Simone hated herself for what she was doing to him, but she had gone too far to pull back now. And Tyler had just appeared at the other end of the hall, surrounded by his friends. "I didn't mean to mess up your plans," Simone said. "It all happened really fast."

"Say no more," Lucas said in a hearty voice. "I'm happy for you!"

But he wasn't fooling anyone.

"I'm really sorry, Lucas," Simone said helplessly. She turned around and slunk away, looking surprisingly miserable for a girl who'd gotten everything she wanted.

Lucas couldn't bear to watch her go. He turned around and noticed that Tyler and his crew were approaching.

"Let's roll, dude, I'm starving!" Derek yelled.

"I'll drive," Tyler announced.

"You guys going for pizza?" Lucas spoke up. "I could go for a slice."

He tried to fall into step with the seniors, but they just brushed past him like he wasn't even there.

"You're the man, Luke!" Tyler called over his shoulder as the guys trampled down the stairs, leaving Lucas standing there, alone again, with the cold realization that Tyler wasn't his buddy any more than Simone was his girlfriend.

An hour later, Nova stood in the gym, taking it all in. The room had been utterly transformed by the new decorations—the gothic tree, the shimmery stars, the stunning centerpieces, and especially the magical fountain. Nova had to admit that they looked even better than the old ones. Somehow, it had all gotten done in time.

Thanks to Jesse.

There was just one decoration left—the mirrored disco ball. A tall ladder stood in the middle of the room, waiting for Jesse's arrival. Nova wanted him to be a part of this moment. After all his hard work, she knew he deserved it. She carefully removed the disco ball from its packing crate and gently spun it. The disco ball twinkled and shone, projecting light around the room that bounced off the metallic stars. It was like a private preview of how amazing Brookside's Prom was going to be . . . in just one more day!

Faintly, in the distance, Nova heard something. A motorcycle. Her heart started to beat a little faster. She tried to catch a glimpse of her appearance in the disco ball's tiny mirrored panels, but the funhouse effect it gave to her appearance was *not* what she was looking for.

It was too late, anyway, because at that moment the door banged open.

Jesse had arrived.

"Hey," Nova said.

"Hey."

She tucked her hair behind her ear and bit her lip to keep it from trembling. As Jesse strode toward her, Nova's eyes lit up.

This was it.

He was going to ask her.

She just knew it.

Without thinking, Nova twirled the disco ball, and the little flashes of light illuminated the whole room. Jesse reached out . . . and took it from her hands. He didn't say anything as he started climbing the ladder.

"I'm just wondering if it's a little predictable, disco

ball in the middle of the dance floor," Nova spoke up. "What about maybe putting it in the corner, and then lighting it from an angle—"

"Nova, just tell me where you want it," Jesse interrupted her from halfway up the ladder. His voice was cold.

"You don't have an opinion?"

"My opinion is I want to hang this thing and be done with it."

"Okay," Nova replied slowly. "I guess the center's fine."

Jesse started climbing the ladder again.

"I can't wait 'til you turn that fountain on underneath these lights," Nova continued, stubbornly ignoring the ice Jesse was sending her way.

"Me?"

"Who else?" she asked.

When he reached the top of the ladder, Jesse realized he didn't have the right tools to hang the disco ball. He climbed back down and started rummaging through a tool box.

"I won't be there," he said.

Nova wasn't sure she'd heard him right over the clanking of the tools. She hesitated, waiting—

Hoping—

"You didn't think I was actually gonna go to this thing, did you?" Jesse asked without looking up.

"Um . . . yeah," Nova replied. After yesterday? And the diner? Of course I thought you were going—with me! she added silently.

Jesse continued to sift through the tools. "I've wasted enough of my time on Prom."

Nova's chin jutted out as an expression of stubbornness and determination crossed her face. "I don't think it was a waste of time," she said softly. "For us."

"What 'us?'" Jesse snapped.

She blinked hard, but Nova wasn't ready to give up—not after everything they had shared over the past few weeks. "I guess I thought we were building more than just a fountain."

"That's very poetic," Jesse said, with that awful smirk she remembered from the first day they'd worked together. "Will you write it in my yearbook?"

"You really expect me to believe that this hasn't meant anything to you?" she demanded. "You don't feel different?"

Jesse stood up. "How I *feel* or how you *feel* doesn't mean anything."

"What?"

"Your world may be all disco balls and celestial fountains, but that's not where I live," he snapped. "Where I live, I'm a bad guy who's going nowhere, and that's the only reason I'm here."

Nova wasn't buying it. "That's the only reason, huh?" she asked. "And what if I tell you that if I'd known how that fire would bring you into my life, I would've set it myself?"

She saw the struggle on his face, the way his eyes darted from her face and then toward the door, but she wasn't going to let him walk away before she was done. She had played it safe her whole life. And she was tired of it. Nova crossed the room in five steps, until she was standing right in front of him, forcing him to look at her.

"This isn't about Prom, or what anybody else thinks, or even about how it's gonna end," Nova said, her voice ringing through the gym. "I don't care about that, I care about *you*. Tell me you don't feel the same way."

Nova stared into Jesse's eyes, searching for the answer before it could reach his lips.

They were dark and cold.

"I don't," he said.

Then, without another word, Jesse dropped the tools and walked away, leaving Nova alone in the gym, surrounded by all the twinkling stars they had made together, and crushed by a blow she hadn't seen coming.

It would have been a small comfort to her if she could have seen Jesse in the parking lot, his face like a mask of pain and confusion and anger as he struggled to start his bike. When all he wanted to do in the world was get away from there, it was as if the bike was fighting him, its engine revving without roaring to life.

He couldn't resist glancing over his shoulder at the gym with a last, miserable hope that he knew he had no right to expect. It was better, Jesse knew, that Nova hadn't come running after him. Because his whole facade was about to crumble, and he couldn't keep it up for a minute longer, not in front of her, not with her eyes so bright and intense, and her lips so full and trembling, and her voice so strong and true.

Suddenly the engine kicked into gear and Jesse zoomed out of the parking lot, speeding away as fast as he dared. He reminded himself again that he had done the right thing, even though it had felt like he was ripping his heart out with his own hands. It was better for

Nova this way, even if she didn't know it yet. Without a screwup like him to ruin her life, Nova could have everything she wanted.

And Jesse wanted that for Nova even more than he wanted her for himself.

FIFTEEN

Lucas sat on the front steps of the school, staring vacantly at the horizon. He was only vaguely aware of the snarl of Jesse's motorcycle as it raced off down the street. He hardly even noticed when Lloyd sat down next to him.

"That does it," Lloyd announced. "I've officially been rejected by every girl at Brookside."

"I know the feeling," sighed Lucas.

"What's her name?" Lloyd asked.

"Simone."

"Simone," echoed Lloyd. "What happened?"

"She wants to go to Prom," Lucas said simply.

Lloyd shook his head in sympathy. "I should've known. Prom. That soul-crushing mistress. We'd all be better off without it."

"Yeah, well, she's going," Lucas replied. "And now she'll never know how I feel."

Lloyd studied him out of the corner of his eye. Should he . . .

Of course he should.

In fact, he had to.

"You gotta tell her," Lloyd said, so firmly that Lucas looked up.

"You don't even know me," Lucas said with a slight frown.

"Oh, *don't I*?" Lloyd asked. "Shy, nice guy, always waiting for the right time to make his move . . . and the right time never comes? Before you know it, you're a senior, couple weeks from graduating, and . . . well, you saw."

Lloyd gestured to a group of girls standing near the curb. When they glanced over, he waved, but they all turned away.

"There's nothing I can do about it," Lucas replied hopelessly.

"Not true," Lloyd told him. "You can change the

future. But you have to act. You can't keep waiting for the right moment to happen. *Make* it happen. What do you have to lose?"

Lucas didn't answer as Lloyd's question ran through his mind, again and again. What *did* he have to lose? Simone? He had already lost her, right?

With brilliant clarity, Lucas suddenly realized that that statement was only true if he did nothing. But if he owned up to his feelings, if he faced the possibility of rejection without backing down, then maybe he could change things.

Maybe, if he stopped trying to play it cool and simply told Simone just how much he cared for her, he wouldn't have to lose at all.

Meanwhile, Simone sat across from Tyler in a booth at the local pizza place, sharing a pie loaded with toppings. Behind her, a bunch of Tyler's friends were playing video games. Tyler's eyes lit up when he saw that one of his pals was about to lose. "Hey, Max, I play winner!" he called out before cramming the last bite of the slice into his mouth. He climbed out of the booth and was about to head over to the arcade games when he briefly turned to Simone. "You cool?" he asked.

She nodded, of course.

Tyler flashed her a grin and walked away.

Just then, Jordan slid into the booth across from Simone—right where Tyler had been sitting moments before. The vinyl seat was still warm from his body heat.

"So you're the earring," Jordan said as she stared at Simone.

A look of utter panic crossed Simone's face. "Jordan," she began. "I swear I didn't know Tyler had a girlfriend when we went out, please, you have to believe me—"

"I do," Jordan interrupted her right away.

"I—" Simone frowned a little as she tried to understand. "You do? Really?"

"Tyler can be very convincing," Jordan replied. "It's part of his charm. He makes you feel like you are the only girl in the world."

Simone blinked quickly, unsettled to hear another girl describe him so perfectly. "Look, I'm really sorry," she tried to apologize.

"Sorry?" Jordan repeated. She shook her head. "You did me a favor. See, I always thought Tyler Barso was the prize. But it turns out I'm the prize. And he lost."

Jordan smiled at Simone as she slipped out of the booth; her smile was full of a graceful acceptance that Simone hadn't seen before in the other girls at Brookside High. As she walked out of the pizza place, into the warm spring evening and the golden setting sun, Jordan suddenly didn't look like a high school student anymore.

She looked like someone ready for the future.

Ready for something even better.

The sun had just started to set when Jesse roared into the parking lot of the diner where his mom worked. The timing was perfect—or terrible, depending on your perspective. Because that same group of rude college kids was just leaving the diner, and Jesse was itching for a fight—the one that had been building inside him since those guys had disrespected his mother, the one that was stoked by Frank's warning behind the grocery store.

Jesse jumped off his bike and barged up to them. "See me now?" he exploded as he swung and missed and swung again.

Of course he was outnumbered.

Of course he never stood a chance.

But the element of surprise and the force of pure, unadulterated rage was on his side—for a moment, at least. The grunts of pain and shock spurred him on until the guys recovered their senses enough to fight back.

Sandra burst out of the diner at the same time as Jesse took a hard punch to the gut. He knew right then that he wasn't going to win this fight. But he wasn't going to give up without trying. If his mom hadn't rushed in to break it up, he would've been hurt a lot worse. Jesse doubled over, clutching his middle, and spat on the ground. Though he was only partially aware of his mom convincing the other guys to leave, it still made him burn with anger.

But then Jesse looked up, and his anger evaporated when he saw Charlie pressed against the diner window, terror written on his face. It was enough to make Jesse feel sick with shame. He couldn't take looking at those big, scared eyes and know that *he* was the one who had filled them with fear. Jesse stared at the ground. He felt like a coward, like a loser who picked fights he could never win, like a deadbeat who let everybody down.

Like his father.

Somehow Nova found the janitor and helped him hang the disco ball. Somehow she folded up the ladder and packed away the tools. Somehow she turned out the lights to the gym and closed the door. Somehow she drove home as carefully as always, observing all the rules of the road. Somehow she slipped into the house without her parents hearing and escaped to the privacy of her bedroom without anyone knowing she was there. With a soft *click* she closed the door behind her, and only then did she let out the long shaky breath she'd been holding since Jesse had stomped on her heart.

It was the night before Prom, and this was *not* how Nova had expected to spend it, all alone, weighed down by a heavy sadness that could only be relieved by a good, long cry. But even though there was a hard, painful lump in her throat, for some reason the tears just wouldn't come.

Nova's Prom dress, hanging from the armoire, fluttered like a ghost. But that's not what caught Nova's eye. Once she saw it, Nova couldn't look away: the glossy, bright Prom poster that Mei had designed, the very last one of the batch, the one that Nova had hung up in her bedroom with such a happy sense of expectation just a few weeks before.

Had that really been her? It felt like such a long time ago. So much had happened since then.

So much had changed.

With shaking hands Nova ripped the poster off

the wall and tore it up as a choking sob rose in her throat. She fell onto her bed, weeping into one of the soft pillows as the torn-up poster fluttered around her, destroyed like all her dreams for Prom.

CHAPTER

✦ ⋆ ✦ SIXTEEN ☆ ♥ ✦

Saturday morning dawned bright and beautiful. The sun sparkled off a row of freshly washed limousines waiting in a parking lot as Brookside seniors all over town got ready for Prom. Dresses were whisked out of plastic bags; shoes were polished until they gleamed; nails were painted in every color of the rainbow; and hair was swept and sprayed into glamorous up-dos. There was a giddy excitement building as the minutes ticked away until evening, when the long-awaited Starry Night would come at last.

For most people, that is. But for some, Prom brought with it more complicated feelings. . . .

Simone's fingers shook as she tried to paint her nails in a beautiful shade of red that would stand out against her elegant blue dress. She could take deep breaths until she fell over from dizziness, but she couldn't quite calm the anxiety that made her hands tremble.

Dressed in jeans and a T-shirt, Justin stood in front of the open fridge in his kitchen, feeling the cold air pour out. Then he found what he was looking for: the clear plastic case that contained a cluster of delicate roses stitched to a satin ribbon. Justin wasn't even sure why he'd picked it up from the florist last night. It was a foolish thing to do, just like hoping that Mei would call. Or come over. Or do anything to let him know that she still cared.

Over at his house, Rolo sprawled out in front of the TV, wearing a tuxedo shirt and formal jacket . . . but no pants.

In her bedroom, Jordan stood in front of the full-length mirror, nervous but excited. She was ready for Prom—on her own terms.

And across town, Lloyd looked into the mirror, too, as he straightened his bow tie. He wasn't going to miss Prom—even if he'd been shot down so many times he'd lost count. In the end, when it really mattered, he'd found a date . . . a girl who didn't care if he wasn't popular or cool; a girl who could appreciate how funny and smart he was.

"Hey, Tess," he yelled. "You ready yet?"

Tess appeared at the top of the stairs, all bubbly and excited in a lovely yellow gown. She skipped downstairs giddily as Lloyd offered her his arm.

With a strange sense of resignation and duty, Nova had gone through the motions of getting ready for Prom, too—hair and makeup, lotion and perfume. She was wearing *the dress*, but it didn't fill her with the same thrill as when she'd tried it on for Jesse. Mei's platform sandals were strapped onto her feet. It didn't matter anymore if they made her taller than Jesse. After all, it wasn't as if he was going to show up.

Nova didn't even try to fake a smile as Kitty posed her by the fireplace for pictures; it was painfully embarrassing to stand there all by herself. "Do we really have to do the picture-by-the-fireplace thing?" she asked.

"You'll want these memories one day," Nova's mom insisted.

"I highly doubt that," Nova replied.

"Come on, it's gonna be great," Frank said heartily,

bursting with pride as he looked at the beautiful young woman Nova had become.

"Why?" Nova asked. "Because the balloons are right? And the tablecloths match the napkins? Is that what Prom is about?"

"Lots of people go to Prom without dates!" Frank said, trying to lift her mood. But Nova just shook her head and looked away.

"Frank," Kitty said as she reached out to stroke Nova's hair. At the familiar comfort of her mother's touch, Nova's shoulders fell, and she closed her eyes, trying not to cry.

"I think this is about someone in particular, isn't it?" Kitty asked her softly.

"I know it didn't make sense," Nova said, blinking back tears, "but it just felt right. Why can't I have that? What did I do wrong?"

"I had a talk with him," Frank said.

"What?" Kitty and Nova exclaimed at the same time.

"I was protecting what we've always talked about for you," Frank explained. "I didn't want to see you ruin everything you have coming your way. You've worked so hard."

Nova stood there looking at her dad, and a quiet sadness overtook her. "I know you thought you were doing the right thing," Nova said. "But you have to let me be the daughter you raised me to be."

No anger, no yelling, no hysterics, no drama. Calmly, Nova walked outside, a girl who had just grown up in front of her parents' eyes. Frank watched forlornly as she got into her car.

"Frank, she's gonna be okay," Kitty said. She wrapped her arms around Frank, and together, they watched Nova drive away.

Dusk was falling when the doorbell rang at Justin's house. When he opened the door, Justin was surprised to find Mei standing on his doorstep, wearing her favorite jeans, with her hair pulled back into a simple ponytail.

"I have to tell you something," she said.

Justin stepped outside and closed the door behind him, pausing for just a moment to brace himself, knowing that it was here at last: the inevitable breakup, Mei's growing distance made official. Better, he figured, to just get it over with.

They sat on the front step, just a fraction of space between them.

"I got accepted to Parsons," she continued. "For design."

"In New York?" Justin asked in surprise. "I didn't know you applied."

"I didn't think I'd get in," Mei replied. "Then I was wait-listed and I thought 'no way' and then . . . I got in."

Mei paused. She took a deep breath. "Justin, I'm gonna go."

Justin exhaled loudly.

"Say something," Mei finally said, twisting her hands nervously.

"First of all, how could you think I wouldn't be proud of you?" Justin asked her.

His eyes were filled with such love and support that Mei realized, suddenly, how much she had shut him out during the past agonizing weeks . . . when she had needed him the most. She started to cry, tears of relief and regret spilling down her cheeks.

"This is why you've been acting so nutty about Prom," Justin realized.

"Prom is supposed to be . . . this forever night," Mei tried to explain. "And we're supposed to be this forever couple. Do you see what I mean?"

"Yeah," Justin replied as he put his arm around her

and pulled her close. For a moment they just sat there, together.

"You know, nobody knows about the future," Justin finally said. "But I do know how I feel about you."

"What if that's not enough?" Mei asked, her voice trembling.

"Look at me," Justin said. He stared directly into her eyes. "Even if tonight is all we ever have? It's enough."

Mei smiled through her tears. "Do you think . . ."

"What?"

"Do you think anyone would notice if I wore my homecoming dress?"

Justin grinned. "Ali might." He laughed, and he pulled Mei closer and hugged her tight.

Simone sat very still on her bed, trying not to wrinkle her dress or mess up her hair. Tyler would be there any minute to pick her up for Prom, and she wanted to look absolutely perfect when he arrived.

Just then, Simone heard a rustling outside. With a frown, she turned toward the open window—just in time to see a rock fly through it!

"Ahhhhhhhhhhhhh!" she screamed as she jumped out of the way.

"Ahhhhhhhhhhhh!" Lucas screamed from the tree outside her room. He clutched a guitar in his hands as he tried to balance on a thick branch. "Sorry!"

"What are you doing?" Simone shrieked.

"I thought it was closed!" he yelled back.

"Why are you in a tree?"

"Well . . ." Lucas began. He cleared his throat as he began to strum the guitar. Just one chord—the one chord that Simone had taught him in Tyler's tree-house hangout. Lucas started to sing. "Simone, Simone, you taught me a *C*, but I give you an *A*. Please don't go to Prom, please tell me you'll stay."

"Lucas . . ."

"That's all I've got," he replied. "I would have written more if I knew another chord."

"Lucas, my date is gonna be here—"

"I'm serious," Lucas interrupted her. "Don't go."

"You're not really asking me that," Simone said.

"I'm in love with you, Simone," Lucas said. "As more than a friend."

Despite herself, Simone smiled. "Love *implies* more than a friend," she pointed out.

"Yes, yes it does," Lucas pressed on. "And one of the things I love about you is your grasp of semantics. I've missed every chance to tell you until now because I was stupid and scared, but now I'm in this tree and you are so beautiful, and if you walk out that door I might as well stay up here forever. I'm in love with you, Simone. Don't go."

Simone struggled—Lucas could see it in the tension in her face and the wavering in her eyes. "Lucas," she repeated.

At the same time, Lucas and Simone heard the limo pull up. One of its doors slammed as Simone's date stepped out of the car. Lucas glanced down curiously, wondering who his competition was.

"Tyler?" he gasped. "You're going to Prom with Tyler?"

"I didn't know how to tell you," Simone said miserably.

Lucas watched, speechless, as Tyler cruised on up to the door, smoothing down his hair. The doorbell rang.

"Simone? Honey?" called Simone's mom.

"I'll be right there!" Simone called over her shoulder. "I'm sorry, Lucas. I have to go."

"I understand," Lucas replied genuinely. "It feels good to be bumped up to Varsity. Even just for one night."

Simone hesitated, like there was something she wanted to say—or do. But instead she started toward the door, pausing at the rock Lucas had thrown through the window.

It was the *YES* rock that Tyler had used to ask her to Prom. She stared at it, torn—

And then she walked out of the room.

The basement at Jesse's house was like most other basements—dark, dank, and musty. It was a tomb for things that nobody wanted anymore, for stuff that had somehow missed being thrown out when it first drifted into disuse, like all the junk his father had left behind when he'd disappeared from their lives.

After all this time, Jesse was going to make that right.

It was long overdue.

He flung open the doors to a battered old wardrobe and stared with hatred at everything in it: work shirts, scuffed boots, torn jeans. They still smelled like his dad.

Seething, Jesse ripped the clothes from their hangers and shoved them into a heavy black trash bag, putting them where they belonged at last. Not even the pain radiating from his bruised hand could slow him down.

He heard footsteps on the stairs, but he didn't turn

around. His mother knew better than to try to stop him. After a while, she finally asked, "How's your hand?"

Jesse snuck a glance at his knuckles. He'd never admit it, but underneath the gauze, his hand was throbbing painfully.

"You know, the first time I met him he had just been in a fight," Sandra continued.

"Like father, like son," Jesse muttered.

Sandra frowned. "What are you talking about?"

"Oh, come on, Mom," he spat. "You married a fighter and look where it got you. And look where it's got me."

"I didn't marry a fighter," Sandra corrected him. "I married an idiot who got into fights. There's a difference."

Without getting in Jesse's way, Sandra started searching for something in the wardrobe.

"*You're* a fighter," she said. "I see you every day, taking Charlie to school, working, keeping this place from falling apart. You do more for other people in a day than most kids do in a year."

"Not everybody feels that way," he replied.

"*She* does."

Jesse finally looked at his mom.

"Your dad never knew what the hell was important,"

Sandra said quietly. "What was worth fighting for. If he did, he'd be here . . ."

Sandra's voice trailed off as she found what she'd been looking for. She reached deep into the wardrobe. "To see how great you turned out," she continued as she pulled out a tuxedo covered in clear plastic.

Jesse stared at it without speaking.

"Even if it fits, you're still the bigger man," Sandra finished. She walked toward the stairs, leaving the tuxedo hanging just within Jesse's reach.

CHAPTER

★⟡✦ SEVENTEEN ☆♥★

The sun slipped past the horizon, bathing the sky in shades of pink and purple, just as Nova arrived at Brookside High. She drove past the long line of shining limos jockeying for position outside the entrance to the gym and found a parking spot as close to the door as she could—Mei's platform sandals were not exactly designed for hiking.

Nova climbed out of her car and shut the door carefully, making sure not to close it on her dress. She hung back for a few minutes, watching couples stream through the decorated entrance to the gym as a photographer snapped pictures. It almost looked like a red-carpet event. With all the attention everyone else was getting, Nova was pretty sure she could slip into the gym unnoticed and hang out in the background to make sure nothing went wrong.

Nova closed her eyes for a moment, bracing herself for the night she'd planned all year. Then she joined the crowd, filing in directly after Tyler and Simone. Big mistake—at least for anyone trying to stay invisible. It seemed like everyone stopped to stare at Tyler and Simone, and Nova knew that they were all noticing her solo arrival, too.

Tyler's buddies from the lacrosse team descended, practically swallowing Tyler up and shoving Simone off to the side. In her blue dress, Simone was almost invisible against the night-sky backdrop. She stood there awkwardly, unsure and uncomfortable.

Jordan's arrival was just the distraction Nova needed to steal away to a corner where she could keep an eye on things. With her head held high and a proud glint in her eye, Jordan swept into the dance, looking more gorgeous, confident, and happy than she ever had before.

The crowd broke out in whispers. "Where's her date?" "She didn't come alone, did she?"

But Jordan didn't care. In moments, she'd rounded up a group of her best girlfriends and convinced them to hit the dance floor with her. There was no way Jordan could have faked a smile that big. She looked like she was having the best night of her life.

And she really was.

Standing alone in a dark corner, Nova could appreciate how amazing the gym looked. The hundreds of stars that she and Jesse had made twinkled overhead; streams of water flowed through the glowing fountain; and the disco ball spun in a slow circle, reflecting shimmers of light over the senior class. All the days and weeks and months of hard work had come together in one enchanted evening, just as Nova had dreamed it would. It was perfect.

For everyone else.

Nova sighed as she snuck a glance at the clock on the wall. Just four more hours and the whole thing would be over.

From across the gym, Ali saw Nova sitting alone—looking miserable—and set out to cheer her up. "Hey," she said. "Nova! You did it! Starry Night. Everything's just like you said it would be."

"Yeah," Nova said, trying to smile. "I guess it is."

"He's a jerk," Ali declared. "Forget about him. Tonight's gonna be amazing!"

Suddenly Mei rushed up to them, looking outstanding in last season's homecoming dress. No one at Prom would ever have guessed that she'd gotten ready in less than fifteen minutes—but what really made Mei shine was the happiness lighting up her face. "Nova, did you see him yet?" she gushed. "I can't believe he showed up!"

Nova's heartbeat quickened. "Who?" she asked, spinning around.

And there he was, just steps behind Mei: polished shoes, pressed pants, perfectly tied bow tie, and that sweet, smiling face that made Nova blush.

Or—used to make her blush.

"Hi, Nova," Brandon said.

"Brandon!" she exclaimed, her surprise covering her disappointment. "What are you doing here?"

"My interview was this morning," he explained. "I was able to get back in time! Isn't this great? I mean, everything worked out! You're here, I'm here . . ."

"It's one hundred percent mutually beneficial," Nova said wryly, but Brandon didn't get it.

"Exactly!" he exclaimed. "This place looks great. You did it."

"Yeah," she said, looking at him through new eyes. "I guess I did."

Brandon held out his hand to her. Nova shrugged, just a little, as she accepted it, thinking to herself how funny it was that just a few weeks ago, this moment had been her dream.

And now it seemed so hollow and empty.

As Brandon led Nova onto the dance floor, she peeked toward the door, hoping for the impossible and accepting the reality at the same time.

Jesse wasn't going to show.

So Nova knew that she might as well make the best of it.

It was, after all, her Prom, too.

Lucas stood on the doorstep, shuffling his feet a little. He reached for the doorbell, pressing it just the way he had hundreds of times over the years, hearing that same electronic chime ring out behind the door.

In a few moments, Corey swung open the door. If he was surprised to see Lucas standing there, he didn't show it.

"My first mistake was thinking Tyler was my friend," Lucas began.

"You hung out with him . . . kinda," Corey offered.

"I got invited to a barbecue. *One barbecue,*" Lucas replied. "What's that mean? That all of a sudden I'm not Lucas anymore? Suddenly I'm Tyler Barso's best friend? I was kidding myself. And my second mistake was believing Simone liked me!"

"She was into you!" Corey said. "At some point!"

Lucas shook his head. "She wanted to study with me. Because that's who I am, the guy you study with. Tyler's the guy you go out with. Which is why I'm here, and they're at Prom." Lucas paused to take a breath. "But my biggest mistake . . ."

Lucas reached into his pocket and pulled out two tickets to the Stick Hippo show. At the same moment, Corey noticed that Lucas was wearing his Stick Hippo T-shirt.

". . . Was getting so caught up in everything I wanted to be, that I forgot who I actually am," Lucas continued. "I was a jerk, Corey, and I'm sorry. You're my best friend."

"Yeah. Forget it," Corey replied, waving away Lucas's apology. "I probably would've done the same thing.

And I know you would've forgiven me."

Corey grinned at Lucas, then disappeared into the house. Lucas waited on the step for a couple of minutes. He heard Corey yell, "Mom! Let's go!"

Then Corey walked back outside, wearing an enormous hippo head. He held another one out to Lucas. Without missing a beat, Lucas proudly put it on.

"Hippos forever!" Corey announced, his voice muffled inside the hippo head.

"Oh yeah," Lucas replied as he held his hand up for a high five. Corey reached out to high-five Lucas back, but with the masks blocking their peripheral vision, the guys missed.

But who cared? They'd been dreaming of seeing Stick Hippo live for years. And the hippo heads were the best way to show everyone their status as number one fans.

Back at the Prom, Tess was practically bouncing up and down with excitement. "This. Is. Awesome!" she cried.

Lloyd had to smile at her exuberance. "Go," he said, nodding toward the dance floor. "Have fun."

"Really? You sure?" Tess asked, staring wide-eyed at the revolving disco ball.

"Yes. Go," Lloyd insisted. "Enjoy your youth."

With a squeal of glee, Tess ran onto the dance floor, dodging the Kranton private conga line. Nearby, Justin lifted Mei into the air and spun her around as she giggled. Nova danced with Brandon, somehow keeping the beat even though her mind was a million miles away. As Ali danced with her date, she noticed Rolo, all dressed up, standing alone by the wall. The sight made her feel oddly sad.

"I'll be right back," she said to her date. "I have to make a charitable donation."

Ali marched up to Rolo and held out her hand. "Okay, Rolo," she announced. "Let's go."

"Where?" he asked.

"Dance floor. You and me. Come on."

Rolo shook his head. "Athena's just running late."

"I'm sure she is," Ali replied, rolling her eyes. "In the meantime, what do you say? One dance."

"Athena gets kind of jealous," Rolo said, trying to let Ali down gently.

Ali sighed incredulously as she returned to the dance floor. If Rolo wanted to live in a fantasy world where a hard-partying Greek-Canadian supermodel was his girlfriend, who was she to force reality on him?

Across the gym, Simone wandered over to the refreshments table to get a cookie. Prom was not really turning out to be as amazing as she had expected. None of her friends were there, and she didn't know most of the seniors. And Tyler was so busy hanging out with his buddies that she'd barely seen him since they walked in the door.

Two senior girls stood nearby, sipping some punch as they watched the dance floor, where Jordan was stealing the spotlight with her amazing moves.

"I can't believe she dumped Tyler and came alone!" one of the girls marveled.

"I know," agreed the other. "It's *awesome*."

The girls tossed their empty cups in the trash and walked away, leaving a stunned Simone to wonder if she'd heard them right. Had *everything* leading up to this night been based on a lie?

Suddenly Tyler rushed up to her. "Where've you been?" he asked as he grabbed her wrist to drag her onto the dance floor. "They're about to announce king and queen."

"You didn't break up with Jordan to be with me," she said slowly, as it all started to make sense. "She dumped you."

"Well, yeah, technically," Tyler replied, only partially paying attention.

"You know, Tyler, all you had to do was tell us the truth," Simone said, pulling her hand away.

Tyler turned around and stared at her.

"Was that really so difficult, to tell the truth? About how you felt?" she asked. "Or are you just . . . a coward?"

As the words fell from her lips, a memory flashed through Simone's mind—a memory of a guy who wasn't a coward at all, a guy who was willing to climb a tree to tell her the truth, even if it meant risking total humiliation.

She had just left him there—and for what?

For a liar like Tyler Barso?

At that moment, the music cut out, and Nova and Mei ascended the stage and stood next to the DJ. A hush fell over the crowd.

Mei took the DJ's microphone and announced, "Ladies and gentlemen, your attention please. We have tallied the votes and are proud to announce Brookside's new prom king is . . ."

The DJ played a canned drumroll.

"Tyler Barso!"

The crowd cheered as Tyler broke away from Simone. He made his way toward the stage, getting high fives and backslaps from practically everyone as he approached Mei and Nova for his crown. He placed it on his head with a cocky grin.

"And what's a king without a queen?" Mei said into the microphone as the crowd quieted down again. "In a landslide win . . ."

There was another drumroll from the DJ as Mei paused for dramatic effect.

"Jordan Lundley!"

Jordan squealed and hugged her friends. She didn't even glance at Tyler as she glided up the steps to the stage. Jordan stood very still, smiling beautifully, as Nova carefully placed the crown on her head.

"Please make room for the queen and king's official dance!" Mei yelled. But Jordan quickly leaned over and touched Mei's shoulder. "One sec . . ." Mei said. She bent her head toward Jordan as the prom queen whispered in her ear.

"Okay," Mei announced into the mic, trying to think fast. "Um, at the request of the queen, she will be sitting this dance out. So it'll just be the king's dance. By order of the queen!"

A spotlight shone on Tyler, catching his deer-in-the-headlights look of shock. This was the first time in his life that he'd ever been rejected . . . and Tyler was painfully aware that the entire senior class was there to witness it. He tried to shrug it off as he walked toward Simone, his dazzling smile at the ready.

"Madame?" he asked as he held out his hand. His crown glittered harshly in the spotlight.

Simone, deep in thought, was jolted back to reality. She took a step beyond the spotlight's beam. "Sorry, Tyler," she said, "there's somewhere else I'm supposed to be."

To everyone's astonishment, Simone turned around and walked away.

Tyler's smile fumbled before a fast, forced recovery. "Jordan," he said warmly with all the charm he could muster. "What do you say? You're here . . . I'm here . . . One last dance?" He lowered his voice as he leaned a little closer to her. "Everyone's watching."

A look of disgust crossed her face. "Please," Jordan replied as she turned her back on him.

Tyler was left standing in the spotlight. There was an awkward silence until the DJ started up another song, and the crowd moved back onto the dance floor, shuffling Tyler off to the side, where he stood awkwardly.

Totally irrelevant.

And totally alone.

Suddenly, a series of blinding flashes lit up the entranceway as dozens of cameras clicked. Ali looked over curiously, and what she saw made her mouth drop open. "Oh. My. God," she exclaimed.

Rolo appeared in the doorway, escorting in the gorgeous and mysterious Athena, who was wearing the dress that only a Victoria's Secret model could pull off.

"Nice dress," Ali said admiringly as they walked past her.

In all the commotion of Rolo and Athena's arrival, Simone slipped out of the gym unnoticed. There was somewhere else that she was desperate to be . . . and someone else she was desperate to find.

When Stick Hippo finished playing their set, Corey and Lucas didn't hang around the club. What was the point? No other musical group in the history of music could match that performance.

Also, Corey's mom was waiting to drive them home.

"Amazing!" Corey raved, waving his autographed napkin in the air as they bounded into the parking lot. "That version of 'War Craving'?"

"The best!" Lucas declared. Then, abruptly, he stopped and stared across the rows of cars.

Corey saw her, too, gorgeous in her blue dress, clearly waiting for someone.

Simone smiled and waved when she saw Lucas.

"Hendrix. At Woodstock," Corey whispered. He reached out for Lucas's hippo head and tucked it under his arm. Then Corey gave his buddy a push toward Simone.

Corey stepped back into the shadows, letting them have their moment. Then he had an idea. Corey found his mom's car and got into the front seat. He rolled down all the windows. And then he cranked the stereo.

Corey sat back and waited. He had set the stage. There was nothing else he could do.

And it turned out that there was nothing else he needed to do, because Lucas took Simone in his arms. They swayed to the music, Lucas in a Stick Hippo T-shirt and Simone in her prom dress, under the street-lights in the parking lot.

It was as perfect as it could possibly be—and neither

Lucas nor Simone would have changed a thing.

"So romantic," Corey's mom sighed from the driver's seat.

Corey just grinned at her. He couldn't argue with that.

Back at Brookside High, the party was in full swing. Everywhere Nova looked, she saw couples dancing, laughing, holding hands. Even Principal Dunnan had gotten into the spirit, approaching Rhoda, his secretary, with just a hint of nervousness. "Ms. Wainwright," he said, clearing his throat. "Would you care to dance?"

"No. Of course not," Rhoda replied, sipping her ginger ale. "That's a terrible idea."

On the stage, Nova and Mei cleared away the boxes that had held the king's and queen's crowns. "Can you believe how well tonight worked out?" Mei gushed. "After all that, and it was just perfect!"

The word "perfect" couldn't be farther from how Nova felt. "Yeah," she sighed. "Perfect."

"Are you okay?" Mei asked.

"Yeah, I just . . . I think I'm prommed out," Nova said as she tried to smile. She slipped off the stage and tried to make her way across the dance floor, but all the happy couples in her way didn't make it easy. With every pair she walked past, Nova was more and more aware of how alone she really was. And she knew, suddenly, that she had to get out of there. Prom didn't need her, not anymore, and neither did anybody who was there. She was halfway to the door when Ali stepped in front of her.

"Nova, you can't go now," Ali said urgently.

"Why not?" Nova asked.

"The fountain," Ali explained. "It just stopped working."

Nova turned around to look back at the dance floor. Sure enough, the fountain was dark and still.

"I don't care," Nova said. "You guys can figure it out. Or, just leave it off."

She started toward the door again, leaving a stunned Ali behind her. Now it seemed as if there were even more love-struck couples blocking her escape. Where had they all come from?

Suddenly a loud grinding sound caught Nova's attention. She spun around in amazement as the fountain came to life, jets of water bursting forth in sparkling streams, the glow of the lights illuminating the whole dance floor.

Nova held her breath. She didn't dare hope—

But there he was, stepping out from behind the fountain, wearing his dad's tuxedo and looking more handsome than anyone could have imagined.

His eyes never left Nova as he approached her.

"You're here," Nova said with a thrill in her heart.

"Wanna dance?" Jesse asked.

Nova didn't have to say a word. The shine in her eyes told Jesse that her answer was yes, yes, yes.

He reached for her hand, linked his fingers through hers, and led her onto the dance floor. Jesse's arms wrapped around Nova, holding her tight. She tilted her head and looked at him with a glimmer of mischief in her smile.

"What?" Jesse said.

"I thought you'd never wear that sweaty symbol of conformity," Nova teased him.

"I thought about that," Jesse replied. "But then I realized that I kind of rock it."

He spun Nova in a circle and she laughed, her face lighting with a glow that put the fountain to shame. As they danced, Nova could see everyone else out of the corner of her eye: Rolo and Athena posing for the photographers; Ali tweeting the latest gossip from the dance floor; Jordan and her best girlfriends making memories they'd laugh about years later; and Tess dancing right in the middle of them. Mei and Justin, lost in their own world as they slow danced to a fast song, his tux jacket draped over her shoulders. And there—off to the side—überalternative Rachel had actually shown up; she perched next to Lloyd, and the two of them shared a smile. They were all here, together, for one last night before the rest of their lives began, before their destinies pulled them apart.

And that was when Nova realized the truth about Prom: it really was a night to hold on to. But sometimes, the best way to do that was to let go.

When the music slowed down, Jesse drew Nova tighter into his arms. He reached into his pocket and slipped the candy necklace over her head. The pastel-colored sugar beads rested in the hollow of her throat, but Jesse didn't notice them.

He couldn't take his eyes off her lips.

"You're about to kiss me," Nova whispered.

"Toldja you'd know," Jesse whispered back. He leaned in, slowly, and then his lips were on hers, and it was perfect, the way Nova had dreamed it would be. It was a kiss she would remember forever.

And a night she'd never forget.